BUILD HIGH FOR HAPPINESS

Edited by Stuart Douglas

BUILD HIGH FOR HAPPINESS

ISBN: 9781913456238

Published by Obverse Books, Edinburgh

Cover Design: Cody Schell

First edition: November 2021

10 9 8 7 6 5 4 3 2 1

A CIP catalogue record for this title is available from the British Library.

Table of Contents

Introduction

If you'd told me back in 1987 that I'd be sitting down, thirty-five years later, to write the introduction to a volume of stories from a very talented bunch of writers inspired by *Paradise Towers*, I would not have believed you.

Like **Doctor Who** itself, *Paradise Towers* has had a bumpy ride. Those who like it, like it a lot. Those who don't, loathe it and often voted it one of the Worst **Doctor Who** Stories Ever Written. For myself, I know it has its faults, both in writing and execution, but I've always felt quite proud of what we achieved in a ridiculously small amount of time.

But this is 2021, and *Paradise Towers* has just appeared in the BBC Season 24 Blu-ray collection, accompanied by a breathtakingly comprehensive choice of extras. Cutaway Comics meanwhile is producing a comic book follow-up, *Paradise Found,* written by Sean Mason and illustrated by Silvano Beltramo, accompanied by audio dramas scripted by me. Here at Obverse, they're publishing a study of the story in their **Black Archive** series next year, alongside *The Wallscrawler,* a collection of my own short stories, many of them *Towers*-related.

And, of course, there's the volume you're now holding in your hand. Some writers I suspect wouldn't like the idea of someone else having fun playing with the toys they've created. Personally, I'm delighted to see them taking up the challenge, and what else can I say to my fellow authors here but-

Build High for Happiness!
Stephen Wyatt

Territory

Courtney Milnestein

Keep breathing, she told herself; keep drawing breath, one gasp after the other, don't worry about the pain, don't worry about the sound it makes, the taste of copper in the mouth, that feeling that you get sometimes before the lightning hits the dead trees and vast waves of the world outside.

She turned her head. The outside world. It must be nice out there, she thought, even though she knew it wasn't. She could count the times she had been outside on one hand, the dim recollection of her childhood notwithstanding. There was no need to go outside, no reason; the outside was dead, inhospitable, good for nothing, a hollowed-out planet that existed solely as a mass of land on which the tower could stand. No one came here anymore, not since the war, and no one left.

She closed her eyes, and then forced them open again, realising the danger in such a gesture. Outside, she thought again. That was right. On the balcony of abandoned quarters on the sixtieth floor, in the rain, she remembered how that felt, the warmth of her sister's hand in hers.

Her head lolled, and she gasped, one hand slipping away from the weight of the softly bleating canister in her lap and hitting the floor, a dull pain in her bad shoulder, her heart tremulous in her chest. Stay awake, stay awake.

In the distance, she could hear the sound of voices, something loud and metallic being dragged along the floor of the carrydoor, approaching slowly, measured steps, high voices, bitter laughter.

Her breaths became shallow, fast now, her heart strained, like the echo of warmth in a tiny animal held close. Almost, she closed her eyes again; almost, she allowed herself to remember the before-times, standing on the ramp leading up towards the transport, the cat bundled in one arm close to her chest, as she had turned and looked back towards her parents, watching the insincerity of their cooing motions of encouragement, the warmth of her sister's hand in hers.

How old had she been then? How old was she now? It didn't matter. All that mattered was the weight in her lap, the frightening animal intake of her breath, and the scraping sound of metal on metal, the bickering voices growing closer and closer.

'I've thought about it,' Astra said, and she had that look on her face that she had grown to dislike, something that she was certain would bud into cruelty one of these days.

'I've thought about it,' her younger sister continued, 'and I think it's right. We can't just sit around here pretending like things are going to go back to normal.'

A light blinked in the dull matte grey kitchen space over her shoulder, as if highlighting the gradual entropy at which she hinted but did not directly address. You've always been like this, she thought. It reminded her of the faint recollection of someone she had not thought of in a very long time.

Emphatically, she shook her head.

'Just because you've thought about it, doesn't mean it's a good idea.'

It was a weak argument, a useless retort—signs of the Tower's decline were all around them, and the girl before her, now so adult in her mannerisms yet so fresh of face, was not wrong in what she said; she simply did not want to accept it. If they just waited for long enough, she told herself, then surely their parents would come for them. Yet how long had it been already? How old was she now? How old had she been then?

They were far better off than some of the other girls, the poorer girls. They had been assigned their own apartment after all, and hadn't been forced to live in the big dormitories near the basement, where you could hear the sound of the waste disposal chugging away day and night.

She was lucky, they were lucky, and now here was Astra, wanting to throw it all away, to run wild just because she'd lost faith.

'Well, what's your solution then?' the younger girl demanded, blowing air through her lips in frustration, her hands on her hips, the loose fitting Perky Pat t-shirt, the colourful print now faded with age making Perky Pat herself look wrinkled and decrepit, an oldster.

Hastily, she brushed past the younger girl so that she could not read her expression, making her way instead towards the detritus of the kitchen, the discarded containers from the food processing mechanism that neither girl had been interested in dropping into the waste disposal unit.

She could feel Astra's eyes on her back, feel her gaze bruise the nap of her neck where the pale skin was always visible now after the bad haircut she had given herself.

'I don't think things are as bad as you make out,' she said quietly, staring at the matte grey mechanism of the food processor, the scuffmarks on the metal, the places where the paint had worn away, the traces of food encrusted about the nozzles.

Behind her, she heard Astra's shrill laugh, the sound of her throwing up her arms and letting them fall.

'Have you been out there?' she asked, her voice rising in pitch. 'Have you seen what's going on out there?'

Of course she had, she thought, prodding idly at the machine before her, not hungry, but feeling like she should do something with her hands. You'd have to have been some kind of rubber neck to have not seen the way things were going, the anxiety of the oldsters, the indifference of the Caretakers.

A small smile touched her lips, faint recollection once more. When they had first arrived at the Towers, the Caretakers had been so nice, always dressed so smartly in their neat grey uniforms, their smiles so friendly. They had always had time for her, never had an unkind word, and, from time to time, they had even magically produced candy from their pockets, even long after such things had become scarce, entrusting her with boiled sweets and colourfully wrapped chocolate, a secret shared, a sign that neither her nor her sister were like the other girls down in the dormitories, that their parents had paid good money to provide for their daughters, and that still meant something amidst the hallowed carrydoors of Paradise Towers.

She jabbed a finger at the dull machine again, faint letters scrolling across the cracked screen asking her to confirm her choice.

Perhaps, she thought, thinking back on those early days, the Caretakers had only been so nice to them because they were relieved not to have been sent away to fight in the war.

'I've seen it,' she said defensively, her cheeks burning red as she watched the slop of the processed food drip slowly into the plastic container at the base.

Pottage, they called it. She didn't know what was in it, only that it was the only thing the machines had on the menu nowadays.

'Then you know,' Astra said with triumph, as if she had won the argument, as if she need say no more.

In truth, she did not leave their living quarters as much as she pretended. Whilst Astra had always been brave, something that she attributed to the two-year difference in their ages, she had seen enough of the wallscrawl and mounting refuse to know that the outside was something to be approached cautiously at best, not a place to be adventured out into. Certainly, she would not have been able to muster the courage to go down to the lower floors like Astra had been doing.

There was the problem; the lower floors, the dormitories, the girls that weren't like them.

'It doesn't matter what you think, anyhow,' Astra said defiantly. 'I've already made up my mind. You can stay here and rot for all I care.'

She heard the sound of her sister's plimsolls on the threadbare rug, heard the thud of her hand against the door panel, the sliding plastisteel protesting in the frame as its crawled open and rattled shut once again.

She listened for a moment to the padding of her sister's shoes on the cold floors of the carrydoor.

Slowly, pottage continued to drip from the nozzle of the machine into the plastic pot below.

She awoke to the sound, although it took her what felt like an age to open her eyes, the slow dawning of consciousness, the instant realisation that she was cold, that she was hungry. In dreams, she could still feel the warmth of Astra sleeping next to her, the presence of Mr Binksy purring as he slept on her legs. Mr Binksy had been gone for years now, she realised sadly. No one said anything about it, but she knew that it was the ugly, dirty cleaning robants that drifted through the lonely carrydoors at night that had got him.

It was dark still, she registered, unmoving in the thin sheets, but the light was on in the living room adjacent, and she could see it burning through the cracks in the door, the sound of someone moving about loudly, knocking things over, pulling open drawers, searching for something.

The cold of the room reached out for her, like a veil that hung just above her and descended as wakefulness claimed her. With a tired sigh, she slid from beneath the sheets, bare feet on the rug, shivering steps to the door. A voice at the back of her head screamed in alarm, warning that anyone could have broken in, that it could be oldsters, it could be Caretakers, it could be the wild girls from the lower levels who she heard whooping in the carrydoors and jabbing at the door controls of the alleviator.

It didn't matter. What could they do to her that hunger and loneliness had not already done? She knew who it was.

Gently, her hand trembling in anticipation, she reached for the handle of the door and pulled on it, light rushing up to greet her with such ferocity that she blinked and turned away.

'Oh?' came a voice from the living room, sharp and cruel. 'Not dead yet, then?'

Slowly, she turned her head back, still blinking, adjusting to the light.

Astra stood before her, clothes and hair daubed with yellow paint, stained the colour of sunlight, the kind of light they would ever know, the kind of light that existed only outside the Tower.

She opened her mouth to say her sister's name, but her voice was too small in her throat, her words too uncertain.

The younger girl turned away, resuming her destruction of her former living space, and only then did she give pause to examine the ruin, the upturned sofa, the emptied drawers.

'Save it,' Astra said, pulling free another drawer, her hands digging through abandoned papers, forgotten photographs. 'I only came back here for one thing.'

'One thing?' she repeated, her voice a dry whisper.

'Metal,' Astra said in a terse voice, pulling open a further drawer, emptying the contents onto the floor. 'Not this plastisteel crap like all the cutlery, but proper metal.'

Standing in the hallway of her bedroom, she frowned, and through the fog of confusion and restless exhaustion managed to ask, 'Why metal?'

Her young sister looked sharply up, her face alive with contempt and disgust.

'Because you can use metal, rubber neck. Metal can be sharpened; it can be hammered into new shapes.'

Still she frowned.

'B-But why would you need to?' she asked.

Astra's face was vivid with anger.

'Because of the Red Kangs from Dormitory B trying to make us unalive.'

She felt a tremble run through her, sickness and worry consuming her, and she reached out and placed a hand on the doorframe to steady herself.

'W-What's a Red Kang?'

'Rubber necks,' Astra snorted, resuming her search. 'Rubber necks and muscle brains, all of them. Untruth speakers. They'd wipe us out if they had half a chance.'

Astra's words didn't make sense, yet, at the same time, she could guess what had happened. The girls in the dormitories had started fighting. Well, she thought, wasn't that always the way. What were they fighting over, she wanted to ask, but she already knew the answer.

Food.

'You should make a choice,' her sister said, some of the anger fading from her voice. 'It'd be better for you if you make a choice sooner rather than later.'

She said nothing, her gaze swimming out of focus, the cold numbing her to the enormity of what she was being told.

Before her, Astra continued to empty the drawers, the sound of clattering scraps of metal a chorus of chimes about her.

There was blood in her mouth, she realised, gingerly lifting a hand to her split lip, looking up from where she had fallen amongst the dirt and sodden newspapers, the detritus that the cleaners no longer paid attention to.

'Aw, does the poor little cowardly cutlet want her little sister back?'

Crowing laughter followed, four or five of them surrounding her in a circle as she moved her hand away from her lips, blood upon her fingertips. A sharp kick in the side sent her sprawling back down upon the ground, hitting her head as she fell. Her vision swam, the pain and the anger making her wild with need, an animal mistreated and desperate for compassion.

The laughter grew louder, washing over her as she struggled to pull herself up, to find the energy, the strength, to stand up, to say what she had come to say.

Brainquarters, that's what they called their dormitory now, and she didn't understand why, didn't understand a lot of the words they had adopted, the words Astra had adopted, but it didn't matter, all that mattered was trying to make herself understood.

Again, she touched her lips, wiping away the blood, and as she once more lifted her head, rose unsteadily to her feet, her eyes met those of her younger sister, standing a head and shoulders shorter than the older girls, her face dirty with paint, strips of torn yellow cloth knotted in amongst her matted hair.

'T-That's not what I'm trying to say,' she said, her voice unsteady, yet her words full of urgency. 'I just… I don't think it's safe on the lower levels, I think it's dangerous, and that it would be best if—'

One of the girls turned away and pinched her nose, waving a hand before her face. She knew, she thought, she knew her breath stunk, she knew that her gums were swollen, her teeth were rotting from all the times her stomach had retched in hunger, driving up bile into her throat and over her lips. She knew how disgusting she must have seemed to them.

Again, the oldest of the girls cried out in sharp, crowing laughter, the sound of it cutting through her thoughts of self-loathing, the girl's face the same mask of disgust that she had so recently seen Astra wear.

'Oh, the cowardly cutlet thinks she knows what's best for Yellow Kangs, does she?'

Another kick sent her down again and she felt something sharp break within her, a moment of agonising pain in her shoulder, the breath drawn from her lungs by the shock of the fall. How had she become so weak, she asked herself, and felt the first warmth of tears on her face, the humiliation far greater than the pain.

Another kick in her side sharply reminded her that pain was far worse than humiliation.

'Little miss no colours thinks she's the boss of Yellow Kangs!' crowed a voice from above her once more. 'Little miss no colours thinks she knows what's truths and what's untruths!'

The cry was taken up by the others, those four words repeated over and over again as she curled up on the cold ground beneath the weight of their kicks, one arm brought up over her face, the other lying twisted awkwardly beneath her.

'Little miss no colours! Little miss no colours!'

Which boot was Astra's, she wondered idly, on the verge of blacking out.

The blue did not suit her. Her face was gaunt, underfed, and the bone in her right shoulder had set wrong, affording her a permanent stoop, forcing her to use her left hand all the time now. Still, she looked at herself in the glass, examined the face that looked back, tried not to feel too much disgust, the whiteness of her skin, the sodden blue rags tied in what was left of the remaining clumps of her hair making her look like a corpse. It was a face she had learn to hate, still swollen from the latest scrap in the carrydoors, teeth missing from sickness and violence—Red Kangs, Yellow Kangs, White Kangs, it didn't matter who; whenever they met, there was inevitable violence.

Every time there was a disagreement within the ranks, a new group of girls would break off, adopting new colours, setting themselves against their former peers in an unending game of spite and cruelty.

She had not sided with the Blue Kangs because she thought they were any better than any of the other groups. She had simply found herself incapable of defending her living quarters against the countless groups of older girls in different colours competing in the carrydoors for territory that offered no real advantage beyond the hollow claim of ownership. It had seemed easier in the end to give in, to join a side. Maybe, she thought sadly, Astra had been right all along.

She turned her head, inspecting her face in the shard of broken glass still held in the old plastisteel frame, seeing only her ghoulish reflection, a dead girl's face held in the light staring back at her. It was not a face that held any unforgotten secrets, everything you needed to know of her was there in the swellings and bruises, the missing teeth, the black eyes, the new angle of her nose, the haunting loneliness of her gaze.

Was this how the in-betweens felt, she wondered, fighting their war in the trenches of their distant battlefield, looking at faces they no longer recognised in the reflections of alien weaponry? She tried to picture her mother and father, tried to imagine them dressed in the fatigues of military service, their faces stained by blood and dirt, but soon realised that she could no longer recall the details of their appearances.

She should feel something about that, she thought, regarding the face that looked back at her, and yet despite knowing that she should feel some kind of remorse, some kind of regret, she could not muster the energy to do so. In the Towers, things just happened to you and you accepted them, grateful if you had somewhere warm to sleep, something to eat when you woke up; what connection could she possibly have to two in-betweens, the memory of whose faces she could no longer conjure up?

'None,' came the word unbidden, her face captured in the glass, foreign and familiar. 'None at all.'

The wind was bitter but it tasted faintly of salt, and briefly, she wondered why that was, before dismissing such concerns completely.

'Do you remember when we used to come up here when the Caretakers weren't looking?' she asked.

Astra lifted her head, her chin black with blood, her expression full of confusion, that of a dog who has just realised that bigger dogs exist.

'It was nice, wasn't it? Just you and me. We were happy then, weren't we?'

She pulled back her good arm and drove it forward, smashing her fist into her younger sister's stomach, twisting as she did, so that the old coins and scraps of metal she had glued to the knuckles of her gloves would tear the yellow of her clothing, scar the whiteness of her flesh, a key turning in a lock. Something to remember her by, she the thought, meeting Astra's hurt gaze, something you can remember your big sister by when you're alone at night, crying yourself to sleep.

'Not many Yellow Kangs left are there, Astra?' she jeered, her lips twisting, lapsing too easily now into the dialect of those that surrounded her. 'All made unalive, right? Guess your friends weren't so tough after all.'

She pulled her arm back again, drove it forward again, the twisting, the tearing of cloth, the scarring of flesh a ritual now, something familiar, something relatable, something established between them.

If there had once been a different language she had used, a language she shared with her younger sister, then those words were now forgotten or abandoned, the gradual influence of the crying, screeching voices of the carrydoors and alleviators being all there was now.

Astra doubled over, gasping for breath, a cornered animal pushed back against the balcony, the wind at her shoulder, the long, slow drop to the desolate earth below her. She lifted her head once more, tears running down her cheeks, neat unhappy trails amidst the grime.

'We could run away,' the younger girl said weakly. 'Just you and me. We could leave the Tower.'

She felt her face contort in joyous cruelty, a sense of elation at being able to exact such vindictiveness.

'Where would we go, Astra?' she asked, gesturing with her left arm at the howling wind, the distant cry of the sea, the dead trees and rotting forests. 'Where would we run away to?'

Her sister trembled, her expression faltering, the pity, the desperation melting away into hopelessness and loathing. She bowed her head, hot tears carried away by the wind.

'I hate you,' Astra said, her voice barely a whisper, her body shuddering, eyes staring at the hardened, scuffed borametz leaf of her boots. 'I always hated you. Everyone said you were so smart, but once we got here what good did all your cleverness do you?'

She brought her head up once more and their eyes met, her lips trembling, her words lapsing into the vocabulary of that forgotten language.

'I wish I'd never come here. I wish I'd gone to fight in the war like the in-betweens. Even dying in a war would be better than being stuck here with you.'

Before she knew it, her hands were about Astra's throat, pushing her thumbs into her sister's windpipe, screaming into her face, a howl of love and hate. She watched as the face before her went pale, the eyes bulging, her limbs flailing, trying to push back against her older sister, but she no longer felt the weakened blows against her face or the kick of scuffed boots against her shins.

The cry of the wind grew louder, her own scream rising to meet it. What was left, she asked herself; if she could not do this, then what was left? Her hands were rigid shapes, bones set in place, the pain in her right shoulder from the fierce pressure exciting a thrill of adrenaline.

Astra's body began to slacken, her eyes dulling. She drew back phlegm in her mouth and launched it out from between her lips, spattering her sister's face as she at last let go, the younger girl collapsing against the railings, heaving, sobbing, wailing into the empty night.

She looked down at the shivering girl with contempt, with disgust, with hate and love.

'Up here isn't for Yellow Kangs, you understand?' she said.

At her feet, Astra sobbed, drawing in shorts gasps of air, greedy for the cold, for the taste of salt on her lips.

'Do you understand?' she repeated once more, her voice louder.

The younger girl nodded, crying, weeping, and she made to turn and then abruptly stopped, feeling the touch of something weak, something pitiful, the warmth of her sister's hand in hers.

Keep breathing, she told herself; keep drawing breath, one gasp after the other, the weight in her lap, the fuse burning steadily, a slow crawl to the reaction of one substance with another.

Nitro Nil they called it, because when it went off, nil was exactly what was left of any girl in the vicinity. She had taught herself how to make it, sleeping in the old library on the twenty-seventh floor once the oldsters had found their way into her living quarters, scraping off the last of what pottage could be found remaining around the nozzles of the food dispenser, scouring the rooms for anything that might have been of value to them.

She hadn't gone back after that, there had been no point, the whole floor had become the hunting grounds of oldsters, the contested territory of marauding girls, and the only direction left for her to move in was down towards the dormitories and the other girls, the poorer girls—the brainquarters and Kangs as they were called now .

She had seen Astra less and less after their meeting on the balcony. There were scarce few Yellow Kangs now, most of them made unalive, taken to the cleaners, or beaten to death by other colours, or eaten by oldsters. Astra was one of the last. What had it achieved, she asked herself, he sudden weight of guilt pushing down against, as forceful as the weight of the cold. They had fought each other for long over so little that she no longer knew the meaning of it.

Perhaps this was how the in-betweens felt also, crowded in their trenches, the bombs going off overhead.

She smiled softly, that old familiar nausea returning. After a while, all pain becomes the same pain; starvation, stabbing, broken shoulders, split lips, it all blurs into one single tapestry of hurt, the same sensation across the board, something you can become numb to, something you can no longer feel.

Weariness was another matter though. Weariness was something to be guarded against, something that threatened her. Yet once more, the sound of pitched laughter and rattling metal kept her from sleep, the fuse burning slowly down within the trembling black canister in her lap.

It dawned on her that she wouldn't get back up from this, that if she didn't bleed out from the wound in her side, then the White Kangs would get her, and she smiled again, though this time it was a bitter, mirthless smile, her teeth dyed with sick and blood.

Astra had been alone when they caught her in the carrydoors. Astra was always alone now, there were so few Yellow Kangs to stand at her shoulders, to tell her what to do, to offer her the comfort that she had not been able to.

They had given chase, those were the rules, the Wild Hunt, that's what the White Kangs called it. In her heart, she had known that this moment was the end for Astra, that when they caught her, they would beat her, and with no one else to care for her, she would die, easy pickings for the oldsters or the broken cleaning robants.

She had felt nothing about this, a strange absence of feeling, the distance between them too vast now for any real feeling to reach.

Yet when they had crossed paths with the White Kangs, when she had been separated from the other Blue Kangs, a shaft of metal driven between her ribs in the heat of the moment, she had found herself enveloped by a strange sort of peace. Her gaze had met that of her younger sister, her lips had lifted in a gentle smile, and she had gently pulled the canister from her belt.

She had never said what she was about to do, they had never exchanged words with the younger girl, but surely she must have known, surely in that moment, as she looked at her older sister, as the tears ran down her cheeks, as she turned and ran, Astra had known.

There was a certain calmness in the cold that descended, the numbness that filled her, the slow burning of the fuse a constant whisper in her ears.

There were only five of the White Kangs left. There had never been many of them, although their reputation for viciousness preceded them. Someone told her they had once been Red Kangs, someone else told her they had once been Blue Kangs. It didn't matter, in a handful of moments they would all be Dead Kangs.

The canister was enough to take out the entire floor, to blow the glass and rubbish clean out into the salt air of the dead world outside, to blast the flesh from the bones of any oldsters skulking about in unoccupied living quarters behind closed plastisteel doors.

This was enough, this was a fitting end, a suitable good-bye, the end of an era. Yes, she thought, that's right, the end, not just for her but everything, all the cruelty, all the torture and pain. She drew a breath, then another breath, and she felt something in her chest, something that was not pain, something that might even have been hope. If she could do this, if she could show them what true horror was, then surely they would understand?

In that old musty library, the stacked books that no one ever read, there were the names of countless men and women who had died in wars no different from that which the in-betweens fought, no different from that which were enacted here, in the dirty carrydoors of the tower. If she could give the Kangs a sign, if she could show the end result of the game they played, then they would understand, wouldn't they? Those old books were not entirely without precedent: a horror too great could result in de-escalation—a decrease, if not an end, to the violence. In her heart she believed this.

She thought once more of the ramp, the transport, the cat in her arms, Astra at her side. They would understand. She knew they would.

Her sight dimmed, her body felt light, and though she could hear the whoops and screams growing closer and closer, Zeneca felt nothing, save, perhaps, a dim sense of satisfaction.

Her head lolled, and in her lap, the fuse at last burnt down.

Doris

Jenny Shirt

Doris Wensley had only recently moved into Paradise Towers, but she had seen so many characters in the last week, passing by her window. It was a place that was never dull, and seemed to have a life of its own.

Although she mostly kept herself to herself, she loved talking to people, and each day she would see two elderly ladies walking down the hall. Her flat overlooked the main square, so when she was cleaning in the kitchen, she would keep her window open to hear 'all the comings and goings' as she liked to call it. One day the two ladies stopped to talk, and asked if she would like to join them for afternoon tea, which she gladly accepted.

A few days later, Doris gathered her freshly baked muffins to take to her new friends. She smiled at the thought that they had been so lovely as to invite her over. Arriving at the flat two floors above her own, she knocked at the door. Through the window, she caught a glimpse of a cooking pot being prepared in the kitchen. She was sure that she'd only been invited for afternoon tea, and thought this must be for their evening meal.

Edna opened the door. 'Hi Doris, come on in, I hope you don't mind the cooking pot, we're just preparing something for later.'

Doris' flat went up for sale about a week later; her neighbour wondered if she had decided to leave and maybe stay with family. The neighbour didn't have a contact number for Doris, as she very much kept herself to herself. She was sad to see Doris depart, but this was the normal thing and you never know in the Towers, people just come and go…

C5

Iain McLaughlin

Minor Domestic Cleaner C5 Alpha Alpha One was a rather unimportant little cleaner. There were much larger, more impressive cleaners in Paradise Towers, and they were the units that were given the more important tasks by Kroagnon, but Paradise Towers needed the Minor Domestic Cleaner units to perform the mundane and unimportant little daily tasks required to keep the place building high and happy.

C5 emerged from performing a routine task in a small empty room and began trundling its way to the next mundane task in another empty room. It didn't matter that these rooms were abandoned. What mattered was that C5 had orders, and C5 followed those orders automatically.

The journey to the next job would require using service elevator 12, and so C5 made its way towards that. It was one turn in the corridor away from the elevator when information was relayed across the computer network that all units should be aware of conflict happening between the Caretakers and the Blue Kang group. That information caused C5 to refresh its memory banks on the visual identifiers for those two different factions. The Caretakers were easy to recognise with their uniforms, and the Blue Kangs, as the name suggested, were identified by the colour they wore.

As events transpired, C5 didn't have time to identify the humans who smashed into it and sent it hard into a wall. It barely had time to turn one of its cameras or sensors to see what was happening before it was slammed into the wall a second time and then a third.

Damage.

The little cleaner was aware that it had sustained damage and its automatic self-diagnostic system had begun to run its checks. The cleaner also became aware that it had not been the object of an attack, but merely the collateral damage of a skirmish between the Caretakers and the Blue Kangs. It tried to relay the message that it was damaged, but there was no communication available. The last data that had been received stated that the confrontation between the Caretakers and the Blue Kangs was escalating and that the Kangs were causing malfunctions within Paradise Towers.

A self-protection sub-routine activated, and C5 continued on its way to elevator 12. It scanned the latest data and selected the safest location to wait until it could ascertain that the insurrection was over.

The service lift rose by a few floors and then stopped on floor 27. C5 trundled out and the lift doors closed behind it as the elevator dropped to its next task.

Floor 27 was abandoned. It was only accessible by that one service elevator. The doors on all the others had long since malfunctioned and the doorway to a stairwell was blocked on the outside with debris. In truth, nothing but the occasional cleaning unit had visited Floor 27 for years.

Certain that there was now no danger, C5 turned off its less important systems and waited for communications and data relay to be restored,, and for its own diagnostics to run their course. The little cleaner powered down to minimum and waited.

It restored power twice, on both occasions to summon the service elevator but the lift didn't come. Instead it glided past, going about its business as if Level 27 simply wasn't there. There was now a malfunction somewhere in the lift's systems as well.

C5 powered down again and waited.

Eight day cycles later, C5 was still waiting. There had been no communication, the elevator was shut off and not responding and C5 was still waiting.

Another dozen day cycles passed without any communication or instruction.

After forty six days, despite being largely powered down, the cleaner's energy dipped below a pre-set figure, which then caused an automatic check on recent activity. The result of these two actions was the triggering of a sub-routine in C5's programming, which instructed C5 to repair its own systems as best it could.

C5 set about following its programming by exploring Level 27, searching for anything it might be able to use. Slowly and methodically it investigated each of the abandoned apartments, taking note of what was present in each habitat and of what damage each had endured. It took the best part of three day cycles to complete the investigation and another two day cycles to assess the damage C5 had received and weigh that against the items available on Level 27 before the cleaner could prepare a plan of action for its repairs.

The damage C5 had endured would have been easy for the repair shop and the work of just a few days. It would be considerably more complicated and time consuming for the little robot to perform this major surgery on itself. However, after gathering all of the items required for the procedure, C5 began to work, removing its outer covering, extracting and replacing damaged wiring and circuit boards. Some of the substitutions were far from perfect matches, but they served their purpose. Some adjustments had to be made to the replacement components or to C5 itself to make everything compatible, particularly in the reasoning and logic circuits, but the test sub-routines showed that everything was functioning adequately. C5 replaced its outer cover and used its newly augmented recharging port to draw a full battery of energy from a wall terminal.

Now fully charged and repaired, C5 attempted communication with the system within Paradise Towers, the system which passed on information from the Great Architect, Kroagnon. There was nothing. The little cleaner knew the reasons that the system changed communications frequencies and protocols. Most were defensive: if, for example, one of the Kangs had hacked the communications. C5 knew it would not get the upgraded communications until it was inside the repair shop. C5 cross-referenced Kroagnon within its own data bases—and it didn't have an explanation for why it performed that act. It logged the moment as a potential malfunction but ran through the information on Kroagnon anyway.

Kroagnon the Mighty.

Kroagnon the All-powerful.

Kroagnon the Creator.

Kroagnon the God.

The data was full of what would be called praise for Kroagnon, but offered no suggestion on how to contact Kroagnon for further instructions.

C5 was still without instructions and with the service elevator not responding to its hails, C5 had no purpose. It sat alone on Level 27, scanning its data banks for what action it should take.

Cleaner.

The word—the concept—was suddenly obvious. C5 was a cleaner and so it would clean.

The first thing it did was clear away the evidence of its self-surgery. From there, it cleaned the corridor outside of all the residences, removing Kang wall-scrawl, applying a fresh coat of paint. It had to install a new arm to itself to do that, but it was fortunate that decorating supplies had been stored on Level 27 and it found what it needed there.

With the corridor gleaming, C5 moved into Apartment 1. It cleaned the floors, the walls and everything else inside the little home. It polished the bathroom, made the bed, did any repairs that needed done and then moved on to the next apartment. It worked diligently, performing all of the work necessary to return the apartments to pristine condition. Each apartment required a different amount of work but the cleaner dutifully restored each one to a spotless state. It had cleaned and restored the thirteenth apartment and was about to start work on the fourteenth when C5 stopped and turned back to the apartment it had most recently cleaned. The sofa was placed with its back to the large display screen which was in place of a window. C5 turned the sofa through ninety degrees so that the display screen was in view from the couch.

Why had it done that?

There was no programming stating that was something C5 should do. But the cleaner did it anyway. It didn't have the vocabulary or the emotional understanding to realise that it just preferred the room that way. C5 logged the instance as another potential glitch, but as it continued its way along the corridor, the repaired and redecorated apartments began to stray further and further from the designated ideal.

In the seventeenth apartment, C5 stopped cleaning. At least it stopped for a time. Whoever had lived in Apartment 17 had been either a prodigious reader or a compulsive collector of books. There were thousands, either on shelves or in piles on the floor or sitting on the beside table or… or anywhere else they could be put. C5 picked up a book, following programming, to understand its weight and dimensions.

But it didn't put the book down.

Instead, it was drawn to the question of why the former resident had collected books. What would be their motivation for doing that? If it understood that, it might understand better how to clean and arrange this room; how to better store the books.

And so C5 began to scan the book, taking in not only the words but the sentences, the longer passages, and it began to see not only a story but something more than the words; a hidden meaning, an… allegory. It finished the book in a few minutes. The actions of the human characters had not been logical. They had been driven by things called emotions and feelings. They made no sense. C5 picked up another book and read that too. Then another, and another.

Over the next five day cycles, C5 methodically read every book in the apartment.

The result was quite extraordinary.

The computerised brain in the cleaner processed the books, their meanings, and found itself doing something it had never been programmed to do. It asked questions. Some of the questions pertained to a story, a simple wondering of what happened next or why one of the characters had committed the actions they had. But some of the questions, pulled from reading the religious texts, were more intense and profound. Why did C5 exist? Humans had once worshipped a creator and Kroagnon had created Paradise Towers. Did that really make Kroagnon the god he had been called?

And C5 asked questions about itself—beginning with, *when had it become aware that it had a 'self'?*

C5 had begun to become self aware.

It withdrew from Apartment 17 and continued to go on with its task of making the apartments habitable and pristine again, though now it didn't see any embellishments it made as errors. The word it had found in its reading was 'individuality'.

At night cycle, C5 stopped work and returned to Apartment 17. It could read a book far faster than a human, and its brain could process thoughts a million times faster than a human brain could. Each night it read and thought, and initially most of those thoughts were of Kroagnon.

Kroagnon was the Creator.

Kroagnon was all-powerful.

Kroagnon was God.

But Kroagnon couldn't communicate with C5.

That made Kroagnon fallible.

So Kroagnon was not God.

Did that mean there was no God?

Where was the evidence that there actually was a God?

C5 found these thoughts fascinating.

And then it realised something which gave it a sensation it did not recognise. From its reading it assumed that the reaction was one of fear.

If C5 was found now and taken back to the repair shop, its alterations would be removed, and everything it had developed over the time on Level 27 would also be removed.

And C5 found it did not want to go back to what it had been before.

Over the space of three day cycles, C5 traced the errors keeping Level 27 from being able to access the communications grid in Paradise Towers. It was aware that without its evolution, it would never have been able to make the deductions which led it to find the errors.

Very carefully, C5 piggy-backed Level 27 into a relay on Level 14 so that if it was traced accessing the network, it would be traced to the wrong floor.

In the time C5 had been alone on Level 27, the situation inside Paradise Towers had deteriorated. The rivalries between the Kangs had become vicious and the Caretakers were equally brutal. A few days after it managed to obtain access to the communications, C5 became aware of an attempt to access Level 27 from the stairs. Very carefully and very cautiously, it added a simple subroutine to the system which would designate Level 27 as 'unsafe'. Very methodically, it began to remove Level 27 from the records of Paradise Towers. It would still exist, but if it wasn't on the system, there was little chance of anything or anyone trying to go there. Level 27 disappeared from the database almost entirely. None of the elevators registered it, its power usage was drawn through sixteen other levels and if a diagram of Paradise Towers was ever printed, Level 27 was absent. Elevator 12 was the only one which could access Level 27 and C5 had introduced a sub-routine giving itself sole control over the lift stopping on 27.

C5 had built itself a haven from the chaos happening outside.

It continued to renovate the Apartments and to return to 'the Library' as it now called Apartment 17 every night cycle to read its books again.

It did, however, begin to experience an odd sensation. After intense deliberation lasting almost two minutes—which was an eternity given the computing power in its processors —C5 suspected that it may have been experiencing a pang of loneliness. It found the sensation fascinating, and so was not troubled by it. However, that experience may have influenced its actions when it saw a series of confrontations while observing the activities around Paradise Towers. A Red Kang lay on a dirty floor, badly injured, but the other Red Kangs were walking away from her, leaving her behind.

'Red Kangs are best,' they said in unison. It was a statement C5 had heard them make before, but this time the robot would describe the tone as threatening. They were abandoning their injured comrade. C5 examined the fallen Kang as best it could by what it picked up from the camera and accessed its emergency medical folders. The Red Kang needed medical assistance immediately.

With what it recognised as trepidation, C5 summoned the sole service elevator it allowed to recognise Level 27—and even that elevator could only recognise and access the level with C5's permission—and very carefully, the cleaner ventured back out into Paradise Towers.

After the calm of Level 27, the rest of the place was… overwhelming with potential threats. Despite that, C5 hurried towards the fallen Red Kang's location, sending a fault routine to the security camera for long enough that it could go unobserved. The Red Kang was still unconscious and hadn't moved. A swift examination told C5 that the Red Kang needed to be tended in peace and safety. Gripping the Kang's collar, C5 swiftly dragged her back to the service elevator. Before it could return to Level 27, it scanned the security network to make sure it wouldn't be seen and found another fallen Kang, a Blue Kang this time, and again she was being abandoned by her own people. She was not far away, and so C5 left the Red Kang in the service elevator and dragged the Blue Kang back to join her. The elevator moved swiftly to Level 27, though it registered on the system as Level 15 and C5 dragged the two young women out before sending the elevator on its way.

The two injured women were taken to Apartment 5, which had twin beds in the bedroom. After examining both properly, C5 worked out their complete list of injuries, and the supplies required to cure them. Food and water would be the most important. Programming the system to deliver water was easy enough, and it could hide their water usage by splitting it among all the other levels. Food was a scarce commodity in Paradise Towers, but there were vacuum tubes running through the entire place which were used to deliver various supplies—food and medicines among them. These supplies would also have to be hidden among the other levels. In order to administer the medication, C5 had to adapt one of its arms. It set the Red Kang's broken arm, gave antibiotics to the Blue Kang for the fever she was brewing and sedated both to ensure they rested.

The Red Kang was first to wake. She seemed surprised to be alive and was startled by her comfortable surroundings. As soon as she saw the Blue Kang in the next bed her manner changed completely. She winced from the pain in her arm as she moved but she hurried across to the other bed. 'Emergency Exit. Come wakey-wakey.'

C5 realised that it had no way to communicate with these Kangs. It trundled out of the apartment and went to one of the residences still waiting to be repaired. It took a speaker from one of the walls and wired that to itself before returning to Apartment 5. The Red Kang was still trying to rouse the Blue Kang, whose name appeared to be Emergency Exit.

C5 spoke its very first word. 'Sedated,' came from the little speaker.

The Red Kang seemed to freeze. She just stared at C5.

'Sedated,' C5 repeated. 'Concussion, broken rib, fever. Sedated to help sleep.'

The Red Kang scrambled backwards. 'Washies not speakers.'

C5 registered 'washies' as slang for its model of cleaner. 'This washie not usual,' it answered.

'How you speaker, Washie?'

C5 assessed the question and began to explain in detail what had happened. Its cameras noted that the human's face changed as it heard the explanation. C5 ran through what it had read of human expressions and human reactions. It stopped talking and then assessed how much information was required, what language was required and whether it was experienced enough with using a strictly verbal vocabulary to explain. There was no point in explaining that the incompatibility in a replacement processor chip may have created the conditions for this evolution. It kept its sentences short, kept the information broad rather than detailed.

The Red Kang understood, though the human struggled to believe what she was being told. 'Washie is now alive and brain-thinking?'

'I do not know,' C5 answered. And then it realised that for the first time it had used the word 'I' about itself. 'I am different. I changed. I think.'

'Not possibles.'

'It is true.'

The Kang looked around nervously. 'This your Brainquarters?'

'Yes,' C5 answered, though the word seemed somehow inaccurate. 'This is home.'

'And you was outgoing from here to bring us safe?'

'Yes.'

The Kang nodded. 'You are not unbrave. We would be unalive if you don't.' She looked at the sleeping Blue Kang. 'Me and Emergency Exit are castouts. Our own Kangs don't take us to the cleaners but they beat us and abandon us to be wipe-outs without protection.'

'Why?'

The Red Kang lifted Emergency Exit's hand. 'No lovey-doveys between different Kangs. That's their rules. We breaks the rules.'

Emergency Exit started to wake, ending that part of the conversation with the Red Kang. C5 brought food and water to the two women, finding that the Red Kang's name was Staff Alleviator.

Emergency Exit was fascinated by C5 and showed less nervousness than Staff Alleviator.

The two women moved into Apartment 8 once they had recovered, and C5 chose to make Apartment 5 an infirmary, though the Kangs called it 'the Doc-box'.

Slowly, the three of them fell into a serene little routine of upgrading the remaining apartments on Level 27 and reading the books in the library. C5 found the company brought a positive sensation. Satisfaction? Contentment? It wasn't sure but it liked the sensation. As for the Kangs, this new life was startling. After a life of constant animosity, struggle and friction, it took the Kang members several day cycles to really begin to relax and believe that they were safe. Slowly, they stopped living in fear.

For the first time, life was good.

The first hint of disagreement came as C5 scanned the diminishing number of security cameras functioning in Paradise Towers. It immediately transferred the image to a large screen, so that Emergency Exit and Staff Alleviator could see it. A Yellow Kang was injured and trying to escape from a large Cleaner. The Yellow Kang was terrified and there was no doubt that the large machine was in pursuit.

'Going to be wipe-out,' Emergency Exit said.

'Must help her,' C5 said.

'No,' Staff Alleviator protested. 'We don't get unalive because of Yellow. She not like us.'

C5 pointed an arm at Staff Alleviator. 'You not like her,' it said, turning its arm to Emergency Exit, 'and she not like you.'

The little cleaner turned and made for the elevator, summoning it and it duly trundled in. As the doors began to close, Emergency Exit jumped in after C5 and Staff Alleviator reluctantly followed.

'Hide-in is safe,' Staff Alleviator complained. 'This is musclebrain notwise.'

As the elevator arrived at the floor on which the Yellow Kang was being pursed, C5 kept the doors shut. The chase was getting closer. It had to time sending a sub-routine precisely, and disguise it as a random pulse of energy.

Now.

An emergency door slid down just as the Yellow Kang limped through it, blocking the cleaner's path. The machine sent back a message to its control.

On the other side of that heavy emergency door, the Yellow Kang was trapped. The safety door was behind her but in front of her were a Red Kang and a Blue Kang. If they had formed an alliance…

'No time,' Emergency Exit said. 'Come with us or you get unalive.'

'And be making all speed,' Staff Alleviator added, 'or we all get unalive.'

'You will be safe,' Emergency Exit added. 'That is not untruths.'

The hydraulics in the door behind the Yellow Kang wheezed and she looked back for a moment. Emergency Exit and Staff Alleviator took their chance and dragged the Yellow Kang into the elevator. When the emergency door opened ten seconds later, the nearby service elevator was registered as having been on Level 15 for a long time. The cleaner set off, continuing its quest for the Yellow Kang.

That Yellow Kang was, at that moment, staring around Level 27.

'Our hide-in,' Emergency Exit said. 'Safe.'

'C5 keeps hide-in brainquarters secret,' Staff Alleviator agreed.

The Yellow Kang was surprised. 'C5?'

The little cleaner left the explanation of its existence to Emergency Exit and Staff Alleviator. It still found vocalising words an inefficient way of communicating, and it was something the humans would do better. C5 tended to the Yellow Kang's injuries and brought her food and water. She was amazed to be given help and precious food so freely.

'Is no to-do,' Emergency Exit said. 'C5 takes care of this.'

Staff Alleviator nodded. 'C5 takes care of us.'

And so the little colony grew. The Yellow Kang —who was named Bin Recess—chose to stay, and began to live in Apartment 9. She joined the others in the renovation work and in reading in the Library.

A dozen day cycles passed before a camera showed C5 a Rezzie in danger. This time there was no argument. They saved the Rezzie, an oldster of over forty named Milly and brought her to Level 27.

Time passed and they completed the work on all of the apartments, except for two which had been cannibalised for parts to repair the others. C5 went back to the first apartments and made changes it chose to call aesthetic.

The colony grew occasionally. A Caretaker who had been attacked by a Cleaner was the fourth human allowed in and he was followed by Shadow. She was young, in her early teens, one of the Vermin, the unfortunates who lived in Paradise Towers but didn't have an actual home or membership of a Kang. They were the lowest strata of all in the Towers. Shadow complained that Level 27 would be yawny, but regular food, safety and being taught to read by Milly made her settle and grow into her life.

The Caretaker stopped wearing his cap and uniform tunic because he knew it made the others uneasy. He chose the name Fleming, taking it from the spine of one of the books.

More time passed and the colony continued to grow as C5 and the others saved those they could save without jeopardising their own security. By the time they numbered sixteen in total there was a thriving community on Level 27. They all knew and adhered to the rules, living peacefully and never trying to go back into the rest of Paradise Towers. The truth was that nobody wanted to go outside. They were happy and they were safe.

In the midst of it all, C5 continued to ensure that Level 27 was a ghost in Paradise Towers, apparently so unsafe that no-one would go there. It also got to know the inhabitants of Level 27 and it experienced a fascinating sensation when Shadow called it 'friend'. According to its memory banks, this sensation could only be happiness. It was a good sensation and C5 aspired to experiencing it again. And it did. The more the residents of Level 27 —C5 included —came to know each other, the more content they became and the more C5 experienced that happy sensation.

There was chaos in Paradise Towers. C5 and the residents of Level 27 had watched and listened to it all unfold, using all of the communications C5 had been able to access. The Chief Caretaker was dead and Kroagnon, the Great Architect, had been destroyed. C5 thought for a moment that it had been right to deduce that Kroagnon was not actually any kind of God.

Out of the chaos there was co-operation in Paradise Towers. Caretakers, Kangs and Rezzies had all agreed to work together to build a better future for Paradise Towers.

'Mayhaps we should be co-operating too,' Staff Alleviator said.

Milly nodded. 'I'm sure we should.'

The other residents of Level 27 agreed.

Emergency Exit took Staff Alleviator's hand. 'With no more fighting we don't need to hideout.'

Milly asked C5 to summon the service elevator and the residents moved away, ready to go back out into Paradise Towers.

C5 took half a second—an eternity given its processing power—to summon the elevator, but C5 itself didn't move.

After all the time spent building Level 27, building itself, C5's world was ending. The humans would return to other humans and those other humans would come to Level 27 to take C5 to the repair shop. They would call C5 a malfunction, not a miracle. They would strip it down and they would end its… yes, life. They would end its life.

C5 did not want to die.

It did not want to be alone either, but it knew that it couldn't control the people it had lived with, the people it had called friends. Kroagnon had tried to control people and C5 recognised that as being just... wrong.

And C5 knew it was better than the false god.

Feeling sadness for the first time, C5 summoned the service elevator.

It sat alone for several moments until it saw the human residents returning.

'Why you sleepy-heading here?' Staff Alleviator asked.

Emergency Exit agreed. 'We needs you to go alongwith.'

'You one like us,' Shadow said.

'And we won't let anyone harm you,' Milly promised. 'You're our friend.'

C5 turned its cameras on what it could see of Level 27 and hesitated. It was safe here. It had been safe here.

'This is always brainquarters,' Emergency Exit said. 'This is home.'

'And it's where we'll still live,' Milly assured the cleaner. 'We're not Kangs or Rezzies anymore. We're 27s.'

C5 felt that sensation of happiness again. It also recognised fear that its friends might not be able to protect it, or that if the truce broke down, everyone would now know about Level 27.

But it knew that its friends needed to try to make this new future work. That was in their nature. It had read that much in so many of the books it still read and reread. And C5 also recognised that it wanted this future to work.

The only option was not logical but it was what C5 wanted.

Along with its fellow 27s, C5 set out to help build a better Paradise Towers.

Lintel

Rachel Redhead

How many years has the old place been here?

No-one can quite remember. Families have been born, grown up and died in its vast carry-ways and arcades. The games we played as children seem so distant now, and yet I can remember those days as clear as anything. Can't remember what I had for supper last night mind, but that's the way life is I suppose.

I was in a kang once, yes I was that young once, a young slip of a gal dressed in red and pretending to be older than I was. Older kangs spoke of secret terrors, but never elaborated. Maybe they were just stories, to stop us from exploring too far? Maybe I should have gone and had a look, but we were kids and all we wanted was to have a good time and a laugh, without the oldies getting us down.

Then I met Spillway, my wife, and after years together she's gone, and I'm one of the oldies now. A rezzie as they call us, with the same youthful disdain in their voices that mine used to have.

The wheel of time turns, but this place will see me out, I reckon.

A Cup of Sugar

Paul Magrs

(For Antoni Fletcher-Goldspink)

My name is Edmund G. Swain—hello!

My idea is to set down a few notes. Some scribbled impressions of what my life has been like at Paradise Towers for all these years.

Just in case.

Well… let's see. My days are often quite similar, with all the same things going on. There's a bit of walking the hound. He needs a good bit of exercise. The four walls of my apartment can feel about cloistered to a creature like Felix.

He loves to flutter and buzz around the lower levels, where the lighting is sepulchral and the floors are sticky and all the walls are covered in quaint homegrown artwork. There's a sharp tang of bodily fluids everywhere. Everything is rusting, dusty and falling apart.

But we take our exercise briskly, venturing deep into forbidden zones. We know all the best routes and we know how to keep out of trouble, avoiding danger and disaster every day.

Most days I go on my rounds. I have a little rota. Ladies I pay a call on, one by one.

I go—knock knock!—and hold my breath. It's always terribly exciting, even after all this time. For them, too. I can hear the kerfuffle and ruffling of female feathers on the other side of the door. Anticipation, excitement… and then: 'Here I am, ladies! At your service! Edmund G. Swain! Come to bring you your heart's fondest desire'.

Cautiously, the door will creep open. A sliver of warmth and light from within. A crack of enticing gold.

Door still on the chain, of course. Can't take too many chances.

'Dottie, Dottie,' I might say, my voice all urgent. Or 'Petula,' or 'Vanessa' or 'Rohinda…' All sweet imprecations slipping from my tongue through the crack in the doorway. 'Nellie, are you there, dear...?'

I know them all. I have a large roster.

Some of them are even older than I. Some of them I travelled with, all that time ago, before we even arrived here. Many of them have gone by now, of course. Some by natural means, others by foul and mysterious means. We never really discuss such things. We never talk about those who have fallen by the wayside.

It isn't good to dwell upon life's misfortunes. What we do is… we just pick ourselves up and we soldier on. We do our best with what we have. We do our damnedest to have a lovely time and suck all the sweetness out of life.

That's how I feel about it.

So, fight me if I'm wrong.

Ooh, to stand there in the doorway. Especially if they've been baking. The wafting scent of flaky pastries… drawing me inside…

I'm a very valued guest in the warm, chintzy sitting rooms up and down the many levels of Paradise Towers. Each visit I dress up in all my finery. I know I look splendid in my silver and lilac waistcoat, my flowing cloak, my feathered hat. My thigh high boots. Oh, I can wear anything. And my ladies always go wild for me. I'm like catnip.

I pride myself on putting on a good show as I flatter and cajole these dames. Graciously, I accept their hospitality. A little tea, perhaps some gooey and crumbly cake. Some general chatter…

'Oh, things are terrible and they're getting worse and worse. But we mustn't grumble, of course. It's so much better here than in most places… Why, in many ways, aren't we the luckiest ones of all?'

I listen to these ladies trilling on like this and I stare at their powdered faces and their inviting bosoms. I stare until they notice that I have fallen silent. My eyes are fixed on theirs. The words dry in their throats as they realise I've decided it's time we got down to business.

Seduction has always been my game.

I kiss and cuddle them for the sheer fun of it. I'll tickle and fondle them for just a handful of change. Then I'll go the whole hog if they cough up enough dough. I was always a very happy lothario.

We all love that closeness and that excitement.

Years have gone by… and I thought the pattern was set. I thought we knew what we were all getting out of it. Lovely afternoon thrills…!

But it seems that now… just lately… there's a different game to play. And I'm about to learn what it is.

Morag is one of my regulars. I've been coming round to her place for years. Morag of the smoky grey eyes, her hair a great big frizz of lilac. A small beauty spot stuck like a currant in her cheek. Today, having given my Felix his ritual bowl of sugar. she turns to me and looks hesitant.

'You seem shy all of a sudden,' I laugh. 'That's not like you at all.'

It turns out that she has a suggestion.

'Oh?' I chuckle, sipping my tea. She's got her fine China out for me. Sponge fingers. It's always rather genteel round Morag's place. 'A suggestion, eh?'

'Something new,' she says, not quite meeting my eye. 'I'd like us to try out s-something new.'

At first, I'm delighted and intrigued by her having ideas. Sometimes it can get a bit dull, the old heave-ho. Even the most ardent Casanova can get cheesed off with just the usual rough and tumble. Everyone likes a bit of spice with their sugar.

Even so.

I'm really no prude.

But there's a dangerous and reckless glint in Morag's eye.

'It's a thing that some of the other Rezzies have mentioned. I thought it was a joke at first. But… no. You see, it began as a necessity… but some have developed a hankering and… a yen for… for…'

There comes a querulous buzz from Felix. He lifts his face from his bowl of sugar and growls low in his throat. He's very alert to minute alterations in the atmosphere.

I give a bluff kind of laugh to show him there's nothing to worry about. 'Well, Morag. Tell me. What is it you're having a yen for?'

I wasn't always a gigolo. Why, in the old days I used to do it all for fun! I didn't charge anyone a brass farthing! Imagine that!

Times are harder now, of course, and I had to start insisting on remuneration for my efforts. I extracted a few grotzits from my clients. Just enough to keep me fed and warm. Me and the hound. Oh, have I introduced you properly to Felix?

He shouldn't be here. Not really. There aren't supposed to be pets in the Towers. But I met him back in the early days, when we were still allowed to wander outside. Can you believe that was even permitted once? It seems miraculous, the thought of setting foot beyond the Main Foyer.

I used to don my hat and cape. I would take up my cane and out I would stroll, through Main Reception and out the front doors. I would be swaggering into the open air and the grand plaza beyond. There was no one to stop me, believe it or not. No rules or alarms, and no actual Caretakers to bundle me back through the sliding doors.

The Rezzies were free to come and go, back in those days.

Though, thinking about it, very few of us did. Even before we were forcibly locked down, most of my fellow Rezzies were glad to stay cloistered inside the Towers. Funny, that. You'd think they knew what was coming. That it would one day become a way of life.

I loved to walk outside into that grand plaza. The concrete was flat as a great big drum and the air was soupy with a distant haze making the horizon look like it was draped in gorgeous rippling veils. Outside was seductive, all silver and gold. I was enticed and drawn out into the world.

But what world was this? Where even were we?

Sometimes I think I knew. I think we all had brochures at one point. We had all the details. But so much was lost and jumbled up in the chaos and confusion of the last days before arrival. Then the fire… and all the fuss of disembarkation… We were just glad to be on solid ground again. Entering our promised land… But we didn't even know where the luxury ships had brought us.

Very few people asked many questions in those days. We simply did as we were told.

Dr Archie asked questions, of course.

Good old Dr Archie.

I walked into the greyish golden mist of dusk and there was a peculiar buzzing noise that rang inside my ears. When I came back home, the ringing was still there. Word went round that it wasn't safe outside. Caretakers appeared to gently dissuade us from going out. Then they were less gentle in telling us not to venture into that noisy, indeterminate haze.

I complied—eventually—thinking it might be poisonous out there. It might be harming me. I have always had an acute sense of self-preservation… and if I had to give up my evening constitutional, then so be it.

But it was on one of my very last walks that I met the hound.

Felix!

I should never have bundled him up inside my silken cape. I knew it would be forbidden. But I did it anyway.

You see… ladies are nice. Ladies are lovely. But they are simply not enough for a man like me. The pleasures of the flesh are all very well. All those crepey bosoms and fluttery fingers. Yes, yes, dear. Lovely. But a man such as I… Edmund G. Swain… he really needs someone he can talk with all day long. He needs someone who rarely answers back.

Felix was the hound who filled that role perfectly. Not that he was a dog. Not truly. He was as close as could be. He was almost a dog. He was the most doggish creature a place like this could come up with.

I barely had to ask him to join me. I saw him from afar. He came buzzing up to me, sniffing. His eyes going wide. We exchanged a few words. Noises, really. Questioning each other in the amber mist of evening.

He was a funny-looking thing. Somewhere between a pug dog and a bumblebee.

He flittered around me on those gossamer wings.

A flying dog! Oh my!

And the next thing I knew, he had jumped into my arms and was licking my face. His tongue was soft and warm. His breath was like vanilla madeleines.

I hid him under my flowing cloak and I felt his wings beating against my well-padded heart. His velvet fur was trembling.

And then I turned back home.

And I smuggled him inside of Paradise Towers.

I brought him into my home with no idea how you would look after or feed a creature like this. He pawed the carpets and licked the corners of my room. He sniffed tidbits of cheese and meats I offered him. His pudgy face wrinkled in dismay. His silver wings buzzed and he zig-zagged about, battering himself against my picture windows.

Soon I was in despair. What could I feed him? How could I have been so stupid as to take charge of a creature—another living being—when I didn't know how to care for him?

Ah, but then he alighted on the tea table. His nose twitched and he suddenly drooled. His protruding eyes gleamed at the sight of the sugar bowl!

He made for the bowl and stuck his thick wet tongue right in there. So now I knew what he could live off.

We all have our special loves.

Sometimes they're the same as our needs.

You can still get about this place. Even now! That's if you know the way. Like I do. If you've studied the plans. Like I have. If you have that kind of keen, analytical mind, like I have.

You can unfold those plans and trace your finger along all the intricate lines and go… aha! There's a way! There's a route! I can find my way, after all. I can still get about! Even now!

And I have to find my away about, you see. People are relying upon me. All my ladies still want to see me. I can hardly let them down, can I?

And there's Felix, too. He wants his cup of sugar.

Edmund G. Swain, at your service. At everyone's service, in fact! Haha!

LOL, as we used to say on the old Social Media. When we used to send instant messages via funny little machines we could carry in our pockets. Remember those? How funny, really… all that tap-tap-tapping and sending things to one another… all in the wink of an eye.

What was the point?

Remind me, again?

There's none of that anymore. And maybe that's for the best. There were such a lot of fights when everyone could send just what they were thinking to everyone else—in a flash! Too quick! Too hasty!

Madness, really.

Human beings need to be slower than that, I think.

We have a different tempo.

Human beings like to relish things, don't they?

And we like to see each other in the flesh.

Really, I'm glad, and it's a good thing that our lives have slowed down.

It suits me and my older body. My less-than-lightning reflexes.

The world has ground to a stately halt and everything is much more restricted. The 304 floors of these towers are all there is. All those nooks and crannies… I can carry them all inside my head.

Edmund G. Swain knows his way around… especially the nooks and crannies.

Am I getting the hang of this story? Am I making it fall out right..?

Of course, I'm telling it out of order… missing bits out…

I think I've been thrown by Morag and her outré suggestion. Morag with the smoky eyes and the lilac frizzy hair.

I think she might even have shocked me.

Me! Shocked! Even me!

'Excuse me, my darling..?' I cough up a particle of crumpet I was eating. 'Did you really just say what I thought you did..?'

'Oh, yes,' she glimmers at me, and out darts her tongue!

But round and round in the telling… the tale always chasing itself… that's the way it's always felt, here at Paradise Towers.

That sensation began in deep space, I believe. It began as we tripped the light fantastic, and one day bled into another and it felt like we were traipsing around in circles… locked inside our gigantic tin can… trying to distract ourselves from all that boundless dark…

Our ship was called the Princess Margaret, I remember that very clearly. We had free gin and cigarettes and we lived in the utmost luxury. We drifted around in muumuus and turbans and huge dark glasses, pretending that our galactic odyssey was just one endless, gorgeous garden party…

Our ship was shaped like a vast wedding cake and we all jostled and languished inside, sealed safely inside its perfect frosting. All us oldsters braving the far reaches of space…

Did we feel guilty? Did we feel strange?

No! Never! Not I!

I was glad to get out of peril. No, I never looked back.

We were old. We had all done our bit. We were lucky to have had our youth in peacetime, of course… and now we were much too old to get tangled up in the space wars and dreadful foibles of younger folk…

No, we were off! We were out of there!

Time to let the younger, fitter ones go to war against… against… whoever or whatever it was they were warring against. We were best off out of it!

I didn't even watch the news reports, to be honest. That's when we still got them. I couldn't really keep up with it. And then they petered out. And hardly anyone really noticed when all the news stopped…

It was all such a long time ago.

What I remember mostly is the ladies. I remember ballrooms and old-time dancing and being lathered in sweat. My head spinning and my ears popping. Games and silliness and fol-de-rol. All kinds of distractions. I remember us having the run of that glamourous ship. I remember all sorts of hi-jinks going on in the depths of the sumptuous Princess Margaret…

All the months and months it took us to perambulate through hyperspace… slinking under the enemy radar… all the way to Paradise Towers.

I remember how, underneath the jollity, all the ladies were very nervy. How desperate they were for comfort. I felt like a fox left in charge of the hen house.

Once we were here, the days became very samey. I won't say that the fun stopped exactly… but a new kind of real life began.

Round and round. All of us living in our own small spaces. We were looking at the same four walls. It should have been novel and new, and I daresay for those of us who were reunited with our belongings and all our worldly goods… it was probably quite pleasant.

But I lived those first months in a completely empty apartment. Everything was rather bleak.

I don't remember being angry or upset, however.

I used to wonder vaguely whether they drugged us. There was a scent of frangipani in the air sometimes. Could it be issuing through the central heating ducts? Something insidious that subdued us and stopped us kicking off?

Dr Archie always suspected the authorities of doing things like that.

Ha! Good old Dr Archie.

I haven't told you much about him yet, have I?

He was always questing and ferreting about. Never at all completely happy with his lot.

'You're suspicious of everything!' I remember telling him. 'Look at this wonderful place! Our fabulous new apartments…!'

Dr Archie would roll his eyes…

He had a head like a rather deflated purple balloon and great tufts of woolly hair sticking out of both ears, but he was a tremendously clever man. Ferociously bright in all the sciences and that kind of thing. I would sit and listen agog as he expounded his ideas during the months and years we spent aboard the Princess Margaret. Dr Archie and I were drawn to spend much of our time together. There was just something about him.

He looked out for me. That's what it was.

I was my usual bluff, blustery, show-off self but he could look through that with one glance. Yes, he saw through me. He knew just what I was about deep down. He knew me. And that takes some doing, I think. To really know what someone is actually about…

Dr Archie always looked like his head was in the clouds as we sailed through the airless vistas of outer space.

'The human body is a kind of wonderful machine,' I remember him telling me. 'It knows just where it's going. It knows what it's doing. It knows all its parts and how to work them. It knows more about itself than we ever will. The body can go about its business and we hardly know what's going on...'

The two of us were bobbing about gently in no-gravity just then. Just the two of us swimming slowly about. I'd never seen him so graceful and... lovely. Yes, he was lovely, when in ordinary life, clamped to the ground, he looked so round-shouldered and rumpled.

I listened to him until he got too technical in his wonderings aloud, and then my thoughts turned to all the ladies on our ship. I thought about them lolling around in deckchairs, wearing big hats and sipping strong drinks. In my mind, I'd be marking up my dance card and drawing up a list. I'd be licking my chops in anticipation of an afternoon's business.

But here was Dr Archie in our anti-grav pool, twirling through the warm bubbles of froth and saying, 'Are you listening, Edmund, my dear? It's important, this... It's about who we are as human beings and what we might become in the future...!'

'Oh, the future!' I laughed, and chased him languidly through the rippling air. 'What does that matter? Aren't we all content right now? Aren't we all happy just as we are?'

He darted away from my arms as I reached out to catch him. Dr Archie kept eluding me. He kept trying to talk to me about his important ideas. All I could think about was my dalliances—my work! And I remember vaguely thinking—I'd never seen him naked before, and I hadn't expected to be so compelled by the sight of him... Those strong and hairy thighs as he sprang and flew away from me...

Oh, Doctor Archie...! How surprising he was.

When we first arrived in our new home, some of our apartments were rather spartan. That was because some of us had lost almost all of our possessions in the last few days of our space flight. There was a terrible fire in the vast, cram-packed hold on the day before touchdown. No one quite knew how or why the fire broke out, but we were all glad it was swiftly brought under control by the robots. It might have meant the end for all of us.

It was agreed that it had been foolhardy, attempting to transport so many tea chests of belongings and heavy articles of furniture through hyperspace. But we were older folk! We had a lifetime bound up sentimentally in those possessions and we all found it hard to let go. A hundred thousand years of stuff... dragging us back, slowing us down as we inched through the galaxy... and eventually igniting into flames!

Dr Archie always suspected foul play. He had vital notes and evidence of his research stashed away amongst his own stuff. It almost sent him doo-lally, the thought of what he'd lost.

After the fire, some of us were left with almost nothing at all. In those first few years at Paradise Towers, we sat in our rather minimalist homes and felt sorry for ourselves. We felt awfully misplaced, with nothing to console us.

Dr Archie went off his head a little bit, I think, with none of his familiar things to hand. The two of us had been growing closer, but we drifted for a little while and that was hard. He walked around looking like he was trying to remember something. Like he was trying to remember everything. He muttered under his breath as he explored the walkways and corridors of the Towers. The endless liturgy of all the scientific stuff he knew, he was turning it over under his breath. He had no time left for a friend like me, or an unquantifiable friendship like ours.

I cottoned on quickly to what must be done.

There's so little to spend your money on here. Money was no use to me, so I started asking my clients if I might be paid in nick-nacks and gee-gaws and sticks of old furniture. Every time I rendered a valuable service round some old lady's flat, I'd demand a little keepsake.

Something that had caught my eye while I was on the job. That gorgeous footstool! Those colourful plates! That life-sized ceramic leopard! Bit by bit I took away enough stuff to fill my home and make it comfy enough to live in.

Dr Archie tutted and shook his head, amused as ever by my antics and my depravity. Then he went off into his own muttered incantations again.

The way I see it, I was just being pragmatic. There I went—up and down the corridors, tickling fancies wherever I went. It was an exhausting business. But no one was left unhappy or dissatisfied. Not when Edmund G. Swain was around.

Up and down at all hours of the night and day, lugging some lovely piece of stuff behind me. I soon feathered my nest.

And then Dr Archie disappeared.

He was one of the many round here who, one day, simply wasn't there any more.

I missed him a lot. I still do.

There were things we never talked about. He tried to educate me. I tried to shock him and I tried to make him laugh. And in the crossfire, there were so many things that went unsaid.

Ah, well.

We used to take long walks together, when all the walkways were clear and it was permitted to move more than five hundred yards away from your own front door.

I was glad that our little span of time away from each other was over, and I was glad to hear his theories again, even if I suspected they were nonsense.

'One day,' he told me, several times over. 'Our human bodies will be able to regenerate themselves. The way that lizards do, or insects in their chrysalis stage. The exact pattern as preserved in our precious, clever cells will be able to replicate itself again and again… perhaps ad infinitum.'

'Ad infinitum!' I repeated, brandishing my cane in the air because I liked the sound of the phrase.

'Yes, yes!' gasped Dr Archie, going even pinker than usual. 'And we can all be forever young! Imagine that, Edmund!'

When he said my name just then, I had a sudden vision of his surprisingly lithe and attractive body turning cartwheels about me in the anti-grav. And those lovely thighs.

'That's what will happen in the future,' he said, and he patted me on the back as we strolled. 'But do we really want such a thing, my dear? To go on and on forever…?'

'Oh, yes!' I burst out, and couldn't keep the eagerness out of my voice. 'But only if we could grow young, again and again…' I held up my wrinkled, clawed hands and laughed ruefully.

Dr Archie nodded wisely. 'You're still a fine figure of a man, Edmund.'

My heart glowed at that.

Then he said, 'All the things that happen to us—wrinkles and bulges, errant bits and bobs, contusions and constrictions—all the things that go wrong with us… they're all just matter in the wrong place. They're a glitch in the pattern of our bodies and I am sure that one day all these things can be re-ordered and smoothed away again, according to the plan. And we'll be all shiny and new!'

I chuckled at his earnest tone. 'Just like Paradise Towers, eh? With its new-fangled cleaning robots and its heavy-handed Caretakers?' Because these were the days when our new home was stepping up its tidying regime and introducing these new means of keeping everything just so. 'Everything that's somehow wrong can simply be taken away, and everything made right again?'

Dr Archie nodded fervently. 'Yes, yes. So, you are listening to me after all, my dear?'

'Always!' I said.

And then, not very long after that, he disappeared.

We were due to meet by the Fountain of Happiness for one of our strolls. There were new rules nowadays and we were allowed to go out and exercise for only an hour a day.

Dr Archie was a no-show, which was very unlike him. I hastened to his flat and hammered on the door. I listened to the echoing silence within. He'd never got round to filling up his empty place with stuff. Not like I had.

A Caretaker came striding up in his grey uniform. He trundled like a wardrobe with epaulettes. 'Get away from there.' He was very brusque. His type used to be so polite. Now they don't even pretend.

'My friend—he's not answering.'

The Caretaker consulted a thick manual he wore strapped to his thigh. 'According to our records, there are new tenants scheduled to move into this dwelling today. Two ladies.'

'But... Dr Archie...' I gasped.

'Isn't in the book,' snapped the Caretaker. Then he frowned very heavily down on me. 'We've been watching you. We suspect you of unsavoury activities. We believe you are mixing with other residents in an unhygienic fashion.'

'Unhygienic!' I snapped.

'You just watch yourself,' he said, in a clipped voice, his eyes brimming with disgust.

I protested, 'I'll have you know that I am impeccable! I am squeaky clean!'

But the Caretaker turned on his heel and was gone. I was alone in that dingy corridor. This was one of the last times anyone mentioned my dear, solemn, funny Dr Archie. When I asked other Rezzies who'd known him too, they just shook their heads worriedly. 'No, no. We don't recall him. So sorry, but we don't.'

'We all live in a collective fug of mild amnesia, in a twilight world reeking of frangipani and pee.'

That's something I remember good old Dr Archie saying. What company he was!

One of the reasons I love Felix the hound so much is that he reminds me of Dr Archie, just a little. That droopy little face. The way he buzzes into dark corners, up and down gloomy stairwells, always poking his snout into where it shouldn't go...

And sometimes I think—it was a year to the day since Dr Archie vanished that Felix came buzzing and flitting into my life with his chunky paws and his molten eyes. I feel like he's my old friend, come back to me in another form.

Like Dr Archie, Felix turns a mostly blind eye to my afternoon activities. When I'm lighting up the life of one of my clients Felix simply laps away at his bowl of sugar. It's part of the bargain. I still get my choice of items of furniture (even though my apartment is quite full by now) and Felix gets his precious sugar. He likes being at Dottie's best—apartment 345 on Floor 156. She always has cocktail sugar. Pink and orange crystals and Felix's eyes turn golden as he snuffles it up.

Morag wants to eat me.

Yes, really.

Well, just a part of me.

'Have you lost your mind, woman?' I stare at her aghast. I'm up, out of my plush chair, spilling my tea.

She looks so demure. She lowers her gaze. 'Oh, oh... It was just a thought...'

I glare at her. 'What's happened to you?'

Even as I ask, I know the answer.

They are hungry. The Rezzies are starving.

Supplies are low. I know that. I know that many of us are scraping along on basic supplies… But there are certain ones amongst us who have stockpiled and squirrelled away all kinds of goodies. Sugars and fats and flour. They are staying plump and healthy while the rest of us shrivel and paint our faces to look like we're bursting with health and vitality.

But the look in Morag's eye is more than just about sustenance. There's something avid there. Something greedy.

'Just a thought,' she says.

This is all about jaded appetites. This is about something new. Forbidden. Exciting.

'W-what would you need?' I ask.

'Not much. Just a little… taste.'

'My dear woman! I'm so slim and svelte. There's nary a picking on me! I have absolutely no flesh to spare…'

As she reaches for her rose-patterned tea plate her fingers twitch with anticipation. 'Oh, you have plenty to spare, Mr Swain,' she purrs. 'All I want is a few little morsels…'

'B-but the pain…'

'We could see to it that it doesn't hurt.'

I frown at her. 'We?'

'Some of the other ladies on this landing and myself.' She smiles warmly. 'We all agree. You must be quite delicious.'

I finish up my tea. An undignified slurp. 'Come along, Felix,' I tell my hovering hound. 'We must away. Morag—good day to you.'

Her face crumples. 'Oh, oh, I've disgusted you. I have frightened you…'

'Not at all. Nothing shocks me.'

'Then… then, you'll think about it? You know, you'll be amply rewarded…'

I smile at her as nicely as I can, and then I take my leave.

That night I toss and turn in my sumptuous bed.

I can hear Felix buzzing at the picture window.

'I know, I know, Felix,' I sigh.

You see, I know that he longs to be out in the open air once more. He finds the perfumed air of Paradise Towers even more cloying than I do.

In fact, it's rather cruel of me to keep him here. I'm making him a prisoner of my love.

I lie in the dark of my over-stuffed room and listen to him butting his wrinkled brow against the thick glass.

What if I were to slide open that window as far as it will go… and let him flutter out into the night sky? He'd be free. At least one of us would float free of this terrible place.

They want to eat me.

My neighbours want to eat me.

Bit by bit. Painlessly. So that I'd hardly even notice as I became less and less of my former self.

But but but, goes Felix's head against the glass. Buzz buzz buzz go his frustrated wings.

Bit by bit I could vanish.

Giving those lovely ladies such pleasure as I went.

The idea is almost appealing… here in the darkest watches of the night.

I remember Dr Archie saying something important, one day as we walked up and down the corridors. Well, everything he said was important… but this fragment from him comes floating back to me at this strange time.

I remember we were walking on a floor that was sticky as fly paper. The air was the colour of shandy.

'When you think about it… about the vastness of time and space and everything…'

'Oh yes, go on,' I chuckled. He was about to get philosophical. I could feel my head start to spin.

'No, really… it's all incredible, in actual fact,' he said. He was chewing on his moustache and blushing like mad, like he always did when his thoughts went deep. 'For us to even know each other and to be friends for any time at all… it is like a kind of miracle. When you set that small human event against the vastness of the cosmos.'

Oh, him and his cosmos! I almost laughed again—but I didn't. I caught something serious in his tone and let him continue uninterrupted.

'We coincide in time and space,' said Dr Archie. 'That's what we do. We are a coincidence. We aren't together forever. Of course not. Or not even for very long. We're each on a different wheel within all the other wheels, turning around on our own little journeys. Each of them epic and vast in their own ways. But we must remember that it's wonderful that we get to overlap at all. We cross over with each other just this little bit, in this tiny piece of time. We should remember that this… this guest-starring in each other's galaxies is quite against the odds.'

Well! I thought. I didn't know what to say. In his own shy, unassuming way, I think Dr Archie was saying something rather nice about our friendship.

Oh, I probably shot back with something rude or crass or silly to dismiss his words, to wave away their whiff of seriousness. They were too much like true feelings and neither of us were good with those. Perhaps in that moment I hurt his feelings?

It wasn't long after that he vanished.

Somewhere in the lower levels.

One day he was there, the next he was gone away.

Like so many others we hear about. Why, it's hardly even a newsworthy affair by now. After the Rezzies are gone, it's as if they've never been.

But when Dr Archie went, I felt a dreadful pang of loss. Yes, even me. Even a flippant, silly old gigolo like me.

And I remember what he said that day, strolling in that glaucous atmosphere with me. What he'd said about the glorious coincidence of existing in time together. Of being in the same world for just a little while.

I'll never forget that.

Damaged Goods

Stuart Douglas

One side of Ken's boot was scuffed, she noticed, as though he'd spent long hours in the same position, with his foot pressed against something rough and unyielding.

"Guard duty," he said quietly, seeing her looking. "You stand stock still for hours, looking out this little slit in the wall, but you need to get your face up close. Ends up rubbing all the leather down one side…"

His voice tailed off, and he blinked uncertainly. His eyes were small and watery, which might be how she remembered them, she supposed, before they took him away for the War. But they were pale blue, which couldn't be right, could it? Surely his eyes had been brown, like his dad's?

Maybe she'd been in the Towers so long that she'd forgotten what he looked like. Was that possible?

"…a damn good life in the Army," he said listlessly, and she realised he was still talking. She'd let her thoughts wander—what kind of mum was she, not to listen to her returned son, the hero? But why was he crying?

"This isn't working!" The lady who'd brought Ken home stood up, and snapped her fingers at the little assistant standing behind her. "Get him back in the van! I said that this would be a PR disaster if the only soldiers they could spare were the broken ones…"

Then they were gone—the lady, her assistant, and Ken—before she had a chance to protest. It was probably for the best. She'd not got enough food for anyone else, and if she didn't even remember him properly…

Trank Tank

John Peel

Jax paused, his hand on the security release for the final door in front of him. He wasn't scared, exactly, he was… well, honestly, he was terrified. But he was committed now to his course of action, and he refused to back down. But he wanted to back down, very badly. He wished that there had been someone else who could have done this, but he knew that there wasn't. Not one of the other members of the Design Committee had the courage to stand up to One Way and Kroanon. It was him or no-one. And it mustn't be no-one.

He knew he was simply trying to postpone his next step, rethinking his decision. It was a matter of steeling his nerves and just going on. He couldn't afford to overthink this. Courage, he ordered himself.

Courage? That was a laugh; he'd never felt less courageous in his life. But he had decided, and there was no going back to meekly following the plan.

His sweaty fingers somehow managed to type in the override code on the safety door. Trembling, he took a deep breath and pushed the door open.

Wind caught it, tugging it forcefully out of his fingers and slamming it back against the outside wall. It was night, but the blackness was lost in the glare of the spotlights that illuminated the construction that was still underway. The construction machines didn't tire, didn't pause, didn't complain. As long as they had their supplies they moved, spider-like, through the lattice of the unfinished final ten floors of the Tower. They were too heavy for the wind to affect them, and they didn't suffer from a fear of heights—or any other fears, for that matter.

They didn't even think about the three thousand foot drop to the ground if they missed their footing. They were robots, and they didn't think of anything unless they were instructed. And nobody would tell a machine to worry about falling off the outside of an almost-completed building. Nobody told him to worry about it, either—but nobody had to; he was perfectly capable of being terrified without any command.

Three thousand feet—straight down—if he made a single misstep…

He wanted to turn and flee; back inside, back down, back out. He wanted to—oh, how badly he wanted to! But he wouldn't. He would do what was necessary.

He would put a halt to this insanity.

He took his first faltering step, trying to ignore the thoughts of falling. The wind snatched at him, trying to spin him around. The wind wanted him to fall; it would enjoy toying with him, smashing him against the sheer walls all the way to the ground. He probably wouldn't even be alive by the moment of final impact; his life would be battered out of him floor by floor. Unless the wind threw him out and away from the building, of course—in which case, he'd be able to scream for however long the fall lasted.

No! Stop thinking like that! He discovered that he was no more effective at ordering himself around than he was listening to and obeying the orders of One Way. He would have to force himself forward, thinking of his own doom every shaking step of the way. He took the safety line from around his waist and clipped it to a restraint beside the door. This would hold him in place if his foot should stumble.

Unless it broke, of course. It wasn't supposed to break, but had it been tested in winds like these? He was trusting his life to an untested tether… Maybe he should go back. It was one thing to go as his conscience drove him—but if there was no chance of achieving his goal, what was the point?

It was simply the fear, of course, trying to convince him of this. If he turned back, it would prove to himself and everyone else that he was simply a coward. But a live coward, and not a dead failure…

Fighting his fears, he stepped outward, glad for the bright lights showing him where to plant his feet. Below him, the Tower was virtually finished. For the final ten floors, though, it was merely a lattice of beams and supports, and the machines that were filling it in. He glanced up, but could see little other than the bright lights from above. He knew that over his head was the framework for the final floors. And, right on top, the outline that would become the immense system of swimming pools, probably the largest in their world. And, right below this, was his target.

The Trank Tank…

It was only a month ago that he had learned of its existence. As a member of the Design Committee, it had been one of his duties to sign off on every aspect of the construction of Paradise Towers. He had once been one of the greatest architects on this world; his designs for municipal buildings and shopping malls had won prizes, and he had a large number of admirers. He had once, naively, believed that he had been selected to the Committee to actually design the Towers. But then he had discovered that the Chairman had commissioned Kroanan to do that. The Chairman had brought Jax in simply because he had been forced to have a local consultant on hand in order to satisfy the politicians. Jax's job, it turned out, was pretty much that of the average rubber stamp. He wasn't expected to ask questions. And he certainly wasn't expected to dissent with decisions made by Kroanon and One Way.

One Way was the nickname that the other Design Committee members gave to the Chairman, and Jax rapidly discovered why. To the Chairman, there was only one way—his way. He refused to consider any other direction. He had been the person who had insisted that the famous (notorious was more like it) Kroanon should be the Great Architect for this project—and that his decisions would be final.

The other members of the Committee were elderly and prone more to snore than to argue. They were happy with the prestige they had been given simply being appointed to the Committee, and were happy to actually study nothing, discuss nothing and—inevitably—do nothing other than to vote with One Way on whatever he said. Each and every time Jax raised a point, asked a question or made a suggestion, a collective sigh went around the board before running into One Way's inevitable scowl of disapproval.

'Things would go much faster, you know,' one of the members had said to him, 'if only you weren't so argumentative.'

'What things?' he'd asked.

There was a certain measure of arm waving. 'Oh, things,' the man said, vaguely.

'Do you even know what you're approving?' Jax asked him.

'Of course I do,' the man said, indignantly. 'It's a great honour to be on this Committee. And things would be even better if you stopped asking questions and trying to score points.'

It was Jax's turn to sigh, deeply and fervently.

As bad as things were, they became far worse when—two-thirds of the way through the building process—the Liaison joined the Committee. There was no warning of this, and certainly no discussion. The Liaison simply appeared at a meeting, sitting to the right of One Way. In front of him was a large-scale copy of the plans for Paradise Towers. The displaced member had to trudge to the far end of the table to his newly-appointed seat. Five feet further, and he'd have been out of the door. He didn't look at all happy, but—of course—he didn't complain. He probably wouldn't have complained if he was sent to the far side of the door.

'This is the Liaison Officer,' One Way had announced. 'We're very pleased to welcome him to our Committee.'

Jax wasn't happy, though—certainly not without further information. 'We didn't vote to add anyone to the Committee,' he said.

'He was appointed,' One Way said, clearly irritated, and just as clearly he'd expected Jax's protest. 'By the Government. I am sure you didn't mean to criticize the Government, Jax.'

Which was far more than Jax was certain of. He glanced at the person, who was dressed in a vaguely military fashion, though without rank or any other insignia. 'And what is his function?'

The man leaned forward slight. 'To liaise,' he stated.

'Between whom and about what?'

The man raised an eyebrow slightly. 'That is a matter of a need to know.' His eyes focused sharply on Jax. 'And you don't need to know.'

'How can I make responsible decisions without knowing?' Jax demanded.

'You will be told what decisions are responsible.'

'By whom?'

Liaison smiled, coldly. 'By me.'

'But we don't know who you are,' Jax pointed out. 'Who are you? What is your name? What is your authority? How do we know you are who you say you are?'

'I have not said who I am,' Liaison stated. 'My authority is from the Government. You do not need to know any more than that.'

'I want to know a lot more than that,' Jax said, stubbornly.

'Are you disagreeing with the Government?' Liaison stared icily at him. 'In a war situation, that is treason.'

'I haven't heard that we are in a war situation,' Jax pointed out.

'That is a technicality. We will soon be in a war situation. The Enemy is refusing to negotiate.'

'If this is an example of how you negotiate, I'm not at all surprised,' Jax muttered.

'You are skirting the dge of treason,' Liaison said.

'Gentlemen,' One Way said (there were, of course, no women on the Committee), 'there is a simple way to resolve this problem.' He looked around the Committee. 'Is there anyone else who wishes to know more about the new member, Liaison?' Naturally, none of the sheep uttered a bleat; they never did. 'Then we will move onto the next issue before us.' He stared directly at Jax. 'No further discussion on that point will be entertained. And I am sure I do not need to remind anyone that attempting to discuss a settled point further will result in a suspension for a week from the Committee.'

And what would they decide in that week if he was suspended? Jax had a very good idea, so—despite his anger—he kept quiet.

Liaison leaned slightly forward. 'A grave new concern has come before the Government,' he announced, in a gentle tone, as if he were telling them of an upcoming jumble sale. 'It has come to our attention that the Enemy has developed an appalling new bomb. Its aim is not to destroy property, but solely to slaughter the population. When it explodes, it will produce a cloud of highly lethal gases that will destroy all living creatures that breathe in the fallout. And these radioactive clouds will linger for years in the affected area, continuing to murder indiscriminately. This abominable weapon is being readied for distribution along the border.'

Jax was horrified. 'How do we know what it can do?'

'Because that is what our own bomb will do,' Liaison said calmly. 'As a result of this development, it will necessitate certain changes to the design of Paradise Towers.'

'But… but this is insane,' Jax said. 'Such a weapon…' He couldn't find the words to complete his thought. He was too distressed.

'Precisely,' Liaison agreed. 'But the Enemy are insane and unreasonable. They will not negotiate in good faith, so, therefore, we must make our plans under the highly likely assumption that they will deploy this bomb and utilize it against our helpless civilian population. Kroanon assures us that Paradise Towers will be able to stand anything but a direct hit from such a weapon, but—clearly—surviving a strike will not help is the atmosphere outside is dangerously radioactive for years. What we must ensure is that the Towers are able to sustain life for several decades without communicating in any way with the external world. Paradise Towers must become self-sufficient.'

One Way said, gently: 'That issue has already been covered, of course. We have an uninterrupted food supply for everyone already planned, and that will be implemented.'

'An uninterrupted basic food supply,' Jax pointed out. 'It will sustain life, but there is no variety. It will become dull an unattractive quite quickly.'

'But it will sustain life,' One Way stated. 'The residents and staff will not have to fear starvation.'

'Just stagnation.'

Liaison stared at Jax coldly. 'That, surely, is a small price to pay in order to ensure survival. Only rebels and traitors would complain about such an issue in a time of war. Are you complaining?'

'Is this a time of war?'

'The situation might deteriorate at any moment; it is difficult to say.'

'Then ask me again when we know for certain,' Jax suggested. 'In the meantime, I will perform the duties I was elected to fulfill—ensuring that all decisions made about the Towers are the best decisions. You do want the best decisions, don't you?'

'Of course.' He could almost hear Liaison's teeth gnashing as he said that. 'And, to that end, we have to ensure that when a war setting comes—and it will—the people sequestered in Paradise Towers are not tempted to leave the building under any circumstances.'

'Why would anyone want to leave the Towers in such a situation?' Jax asked, incredulously. 'They would have to be insane to even think it.'

'And if they have been in isolation for months—perhaps even years—don't you think it is possible that some residents might not become insane?'

'Besides which,' One Way said smoothly, 'you know what people are like—especially young people. The inhabitants of the Towers will be mostly female, of course, as most patriotic men will be combatants. Women can be… unreliable in their thinking.'

That infuriated Jax. 'Women are as capable of logical, rational decisions as men are,' he said, angrily.

One Way waved a dismissive hand. 'That is as it may be. But when under pressure, they give way to their non-logical desires. It is why we have no female Committee members. Surely even you, Jax, would agree that we must protect our feminine population?'

'Even from themselves?' he asked, sarcastically.

'Quite so,' One Way replied, completely missing the sarcasm. 'And groups of younger women—barely more than children—have a tendency to rebel. If they are told that they cannot do something… Well, then, the temptation will inevitably be to do that which is specifically forbidden.'

'And that cannot be allowed,' Liaison added. 'If even one person were to breach the safety perimeter, it would doom the rest of the inhabitants—residents and staff alike.'

Jax scowled. 'What are you proposing?' he asked, incredulously. 'Locking and sealing the doors once the inhabitants are inside?'

'That was considered,' Liaison admitted. 'But we had to take into account that—even among a population of females—there might be one or two who were intelligent enough to find some way around such a barrier.'

'Insane enough to want to break out, but sane enough to achieve it?' Jax shook his head incredulously.

'You think such a scenario is impossible then? You—who champion the intelligence of women?' One Way asked.

'I should think it virtually impossible.'

'But only virtually,' Liaison said smoothly. 'I think that the rest of us would agree that we cannot simply take a chance like that. We must create a situation where it is completely impossible.'

Jax was starting to dread where this was heading. 'And you have an alternative solution?' he prompted.

'Indeed we do,' Liaison answered with a tight smile. He unrolled a new blueprint onto the large table. 'Gentlemen, allow me to inform you all about the Trank Tank…'

This was insane. The 'this' referred both to what he was doing, and also what the Committee was doing. He wished he had some other option, but events had moved too quickly to allow for any alternatives. He had no other choice than to make this perilous attempt to set things right. The Committee—predictably, sadly—had agreed to everything Liaison had said, and completely ignored his protests. He had been urged to go along with the majority, but capitulating like that was unthinkable to him.

As a result, here he was, in the middle of the night, perched precariously on a cross beam three thousand feet above sane and solid ground. His only company (if you could call it that) was the small army of worker machines that were tirelessly continuing with the construction of the final ten floors of the first Paradise Tower. In a matter of days this would be enclosed and flats and corridors would have taken the place of these bare beams. If he could have afforded to wait another week—or even two—then he could have made this journey in comfort. But in two weeks this area would be filled with workers and he would have no chance to slip through unobserved. The construction robots paid him no attention; they simply executed their orders, and had neither interest nor initiative to deal with anything outside of their programming.

The wind whipped at him, trying to blow him from the safety of the perch he had reached. One false step, and he might fall, unless his safety line held. He hoped it would hold—he'd been assured that it would—but now that he was out here in this wind his confidence faltered. Despite the cold, his palms were sweaty—from fear, not heat. He touched the stud on his belt that released the end of his line and reeled it back in. It clicked back into place, and for a moment, the only thing holding him in place was his left arm, wrapped around an upright. His trembling right hand released the end of the line, and he wrapped it around the upright. It took him three attempts to click the lock over the line and pull it tight. Slowly, fighting down the fear, he edged out along the horizontal beam. The wind whipped through his clothing like a thief after a wallet. He shook from the forces involved, and had a moment of sheer panic as he feared he was about to be snatched from the bar and sent hurtling 300 floors to his death. In panic, he reached out for the next upright. His fingers brushed it, but he couldn't get a grip. He had to force himself to shuffle forward so that he could finally grip it and drag his shaking body to embrace it.

He was thankful for the lights shining down at him. He could see nothing outside of their cones of light, so the ground was totally invisible to him. He didn't think he would have had the courage to attempt this if he could see just how far he might fall and be able to picture it. As bad as it was now, it would have been immensely worse in daylight.

He had his left arm wrapped about the upright, locking his grip. Then he pressed the release stud, and felt the safety line whipping back into his belt again. He breathed deeply of the cold air, fighting down the panic and forcing himself to consider the next section he had to cross. How long would he be able to endure this terror? Long enough to finish the job? Or would he suffer a heart attack from all the strain? Or miss a step, and fall, putting enough strain on his safety rope to break it and plummet to his death?

No! He couldn't think about that!

He wrapped the end of the line about the upright and with trembling fingers snapped it closed. Time to take another few steps. Time to stop thinking about death. Think only about the Trank Tank…

Liaison looked at the members of the Committee. It was just a glance at most of them, and a slightly longer one at One Way. Then he stared directly at Jax and held his gaze. It was an old trick, of course, to see who would break the gaze first. It was also pointless, because Jax wasn't trying to score any points. Liaison had already demonstrated that Jax was alone in opposing him. So Jax just sighed and raised his eyes to look at the ceiling. It was enough to make the other man convinced that he had won the issue, so he smirked and then began talking.

'We will have to ensure that the inhabitants of the Towers will not even think about leaving them. With the very youngest, this will not really be a problem—they won't even be able to recall that there is anything beyond Paradise Towers. To them, it will always be what they know it—their entire world.

'With those who are slightly older—teenagers—we will have to be a little more creative. We need to foster a feeling of interdependence—of belonging. What has been proposed is that they be encouraged to form cliques or teams.'

'Proposed by whom?' Jax asked. 'I was under the impression that it was the responsibility of the Committee to propose and implement proposals such as that.'

'Proposed by experts,' Liaison said, slightly annoyed. 'I assume that you're not so stubborn or insistent on getting your own way that you will ignore the advice of experts?'

'Of course we aren't,' One Way said hastily. 'We are always willing to listen to experts.'

'But we haven't heard anything from experts,' Jax pointed out. 'Just him telling us that he has. I think we should call these experts to testify before the Committee so that we can judge the extent of their expertise and how they reached these conclusions.'

'But that would simply be a complete waste of time,' Liaison said smoothly. 'We have had to suffer through endless hours of talk that I wouldn't wish to inflict on you gentlemen, just so you'd reach the same inevitable conclusion anyway.'

'Quite right,' muttered one of the older members. 'Waste of our time and theirs.'

'How do we know that?' Jax asked. But he could see from the set faces about him that nobody else even cared. 'If you're willing to just accept this, then what are you even here for?'

Liaison sighed. 'Very well, I will accept a majority vote on this issue. How many of you wish to have these experts come to testify before you for several weeks?' As he had expected, Jax was the only person to raise his hand. 'I'm sorry,' Liaison said to him (clearly not at all sorry). 'You have been out-voted.' He looked a little confused. 'Now, where was I?'

'Cliques or teams,' One Way offered helpfully.

'Right. I'm sure you'll all agree that a little healthy competition is jolly good for the youngsters. The experts' idea is that we form three teams, with team colours. They will be encouraged to compete healthily with one another, and they will be awarded small prizes for those who achieve the most points. It will encourage team spirit and solidarity, as well as healthy exercise and friendly competition.'

'And what if it gets out of hand?' Jax asked. 'I mean, I agree that a little friendly rivalry is a nice idea—but what will you do if it doesn't remain quite so friendly? Don't they need a little guidance from older and wiser heads?'

One Way glared at him. 'You know perfectly well that there will be no citizens above the age of eighteen until we reach retirees. The adult citizens are required for their contribution to the War Effort. They will be housed elsewhere, and not in Paradise Towers.'

'Except for the Caretakers,' one of the Committee members pointed out. 'They will be men of median age. Maybe they could oversee all these blasted girls?'

'The Caretakers will have plenty of work to do keeping Paradise Towers operating at peak efficiency,' Liaison said smoothly. 'We cannot ask them to do even more work.' He smiled, which was not a particularly pleasant sight. 'Besides which, such oversight will be unnecessary. We have other methods to control exuberance or high spirits. I will come to this in a moment. The final group of residents in the Towers will be the senior citizens, who will be almost entirely older women. They will be easy to deal with—we shall encourage them to form book clubs, knitting circles—perhaps even cookery classes. That should keep them all out of trouble, as well as encouraging community spirit and exercising their intellects.'

'They might get a little bored with all of that,' Jax commented. 'Especially if they have to stay indoors for any length of time. Like years, if a bomb is dropped nearby.'

Liaison smiled rather smugly. 'Which is why Governmental advisors have evolved the concept of the Trank Tank. We have anticipated such problems as you have raised.'

Jax frowned. 'The what? I don't recall that being in the plans.'

'It was decided not to make this public,' Liaison replied. 'It was feared that there might be some… misunderstanding over the issue.'

This didn't sound good. 'Perhaps you'd better tell us all about it?' he suggested. 'So that we, at least, might understand it properly.'

'If you will just allow me to speak, that is precisely what I was about to do.' Liaison looked slowly around the Committee once more, clearly gauging the attention level of the members. Again, he finished by looking directly at Jax—clearly deciding he would be the trouble-maker once again. 'The experts all agreed that what was needed was a method of keeping undesirable thoughts to a minimum. This would solve the problems that have been mentioned—that rivalry between the teenage girls might get out of hand, or the elderly women might get bored with their planned activities. The experts all decided that what would be required was a little chemical assistance to prevent unpleasantness.'

This was all double-talk, but Jax had no problem is seeing what was actually being suggested. 'You want to drug the population of the Towers to keep them tranquil and unable to revolt against anything they dislike?'

'I wouldn't put it quite like that,' Liaison replied.

'I would.' Jax stared at the man. 'Mind control through drugs. It's pretty clear. And absolutely appalling.'

'We cannot take chances with the residents' lives,' One Way said. 'We must ensure compliance, and the best way to achieve this is through mild medication.'

'So—you knew about this part of the plan all along, and kept it to yourself?' Jax asked, angrily.

'Unlike some people, I can judge my duty and make decisions for the common good,' One Way said stiffly.

'And did you make this decision under your own power, or were you assisted by mild medication?'

One Way glowered at him. 'The medication will be for the residents only, and strictly for their own good.'

One of the other Committee members leaned forward. 'How will this medication be administered? It obviously can't be done on a voluntary basis because we couldn't afford any of the residents to decide to opt out.'

Jax was disappointed, but not overly surprised that some of the Committee would accept the idea so easily. Maybe the same drug had been placed in their bottled water? If the powers-that-be deemed it necessary for the residents of Paradise Towers to be drugged, perhaps they had also decided it might be better for the Committee, too, to be sedated. Then again, in the case of his fellow members, there didn't seem to be much need to drug them into acceptance. And, clearly, he himself hadn't been medicated into acceptance. No, the Committee were just sheep.

'The residents, obviously, will not be informed of this contingency,' Liaison said in reply to the question. 'It would only cause… issues. The medications will be added automatically to all of the drinking water for the Towers.' He tapped a place near the top of the plans. 'The tank holding them will be fixed in place just below the swimming pool complex. Some wag on the advisory board labelled it the Trank Tank and the name stuck. There will be a mechanism ensuring a regular flow of a very low level sedative; the Tank will be self-sustaining for a period of twenty years.'

'Am I the only one who thinks that this is an abhorrent idea?' Jax demanded. 'To drug our fellow citizens in order to force them to calmly accept whatever they are ordered to do?' He scowled as he looked around at his fellow board members, who uniformly refused to meet his gaze. It was obvious that none of them wanted to raise a stink about the issue. Sheep they were, and they simply didn't have the will or gumption to fight for anything. They were willing to go along with whatever they were told.

'You seem to be missing the point,' Liaison said. 'This is a necessary evil, without which we could have very serious—or even fatal—consequences facing our fellow citizens. It is our solemn duty to do whatever we can to alleviate any such problems.' He stared pointedly at Jax. 'It is unpatriotic to oppose the authorized plans. I am sure that you would not wish to seem to be a non-patriot, would you?'

'Oh, you like your buzz-words, don't you?' Jax asked. 'You're trying to pretend that an honest disgust with your nasty little scheme is somehow unpatriotic. But this scheme to drug our fellow citizens without their knowledge or informed consent is what is truly unpatriotic. People have a right to know what is happening, and then to decide for themselves if they wish to acquiesce.'

'Not in times of war,' snapped Liaison. 'Military secrets must be kept.'

'This is a civilian project,' Jax snapped. 'Not a military one.'

'In times of war, all projects are military projects.'

'So—war has been declared, has it?' Jax asked. 'Are you officially informing us of this fact now?'

Liaison looked annoyed. 'War has not been officially declared,' he admitted. 'But it is imminent. Do you seriously think that the Enemy will announce that they're starting to attack us before they do? No, they will attack first and declare war afterwards. And we will do the same once we can apply an advantage.'

'So, we are only unofficially at war,' Jax said. 'Then I can't be officially unpatriotic, can I?' He glared at the man. 'But I can be officially against this plan—and I am. This is an appalling idea, and I want this entire Trank Tank idea halted at once.'

'That is not going to happen,' One Way said, smoothly. 'As you keep insisting, we are in a Democracy, and the majority rule. And you are in a minority—a minority of one, in fact. You are out-voted. Now, let us move –'

'I haven't been out-voted on anything,' Jax objected. 'To be out-voted, there has to be a vote. I would like there to be a vote taken and recorded. I want every coward who refuses to stand up for the rights of our vulnerable fellow citizens to go on record.'

One Way glanced quickly at Liaison and then nodded. 'Very well—as I said, we are a Democracy, and it is your right to call for a vote.' He looked around the table. 'Everyone who opposes the use of the Trank Tank please raise your hand.'

Only Jax did so, of course. Everyone else other than One Way and Liaison carefully looked at the table, the blueprints, the ceiling… Anywhere but at Jax.

'Settled,' Liaison said, with satisfaction. 'Enough nonsense—let's get on with it.'

But it wasn't settled, of course. One Way and Liaison were the driving forces, and the rest of the Committee did as they were instructed. They already behaved as if they'd been spoon-fed the sedative. They were terrified of rocking the boat—but Liaison was crazy if he thought that Jax could be so easily led or intimidated into acquiescence. Jax had brooded about the issue after the meeting was dismissed. Perhaps the cowards would go along with whatever they were told to, but he wouldn't. Right was right, and wrong was wrong—and this issue was utterly and evilly wrong. It had to be prevented, and Jax knew that he was the only person who could or would do anything about it.

It wouldn't be simple, of course. In fact, it would have to be very subtle. If the Trank Tank were simply to be sabotaged, then Liaison would just have Jax arrested and the Tank repaired. No, he had to prevent it from working after it was declared functional. It couldn't be just a matter of drilling a hole in the Tank so the sedative would all leak out. Something a lot cleverer was called for.

So he studied the schematics, and evolved his plan. The concept of the Trank Tank was that a slow drip of tranquilizer would be fed continually into the drinking water supply of Paradise Towers. A small mechanism was designed to regulate this drip. Jax had a friend who was a mechanical genius—they had worked together on several successful projects—and his friend had assured him that it would not be a problem at all to design a different mechanism that (to all appearances) would be identical to the original, but that would have just a small addition… His friend took a week to construct it, but it was perfect. It really was identical to the original, but there was a very tiny radio transmitter inside it. Once the official trial of the trank feed was completed, a miniaturized hand control that Jax was given could be employed to simply shut the feed down.

Of course, that still left one not-so-slight problem: substituting the new control unit for the old.

It couldn't be done in the daytime, because the workmen and construction heads would see the substitution. That meant it must be switched at night, when only the robotic workers were present. They would ignore any humans, because they were not programmed as guards, only as workers. They would simply continue with their assigned tasks, and ignore anything else as irrelevant.

For once, the idea that he would be considered irrelevant actually cheered Jax up.

And that was why he was here, now, clinging frantically to an upright, while the wind did its utmost to toss him 300 stories to the eager ground below. When he had informed his friend of what he planned, the man had designed him a climbing suit. 'You're crazy to do this,' his friend had said. 'But I'll do my best to make it as safe as possible for you.' He had stared at Jax. 'Of course, safe is a terribly relative word in this situation. One slip, and it's a long, long way down. You'll have plenty of time to realize your lunacy.'

The 'suit' was actually more of a harness—there was the rope mechanism at his waist to keep him anchored to the uprights, lessening the chance of the winds blowing him to his doom. But then there would be the climb vertically to where the tank was positioned, which required a different gadget…

He realized that he was now in a position to begin the climb up to the tank. He looked upwards. The bright lights made it difficult to discern anything, but he was sure that the bulk of the frame for the pools were directly above him. And—though he couldn't make out any details—that meant that the Trank Tank had to be just below the frame.

It had been difficult and terrifying enough just shuffling around the framework on the one level; the climb was going to be much, much worse. But he was committed to his course of action now, and couldn't back down. He had to prevent those sedatives being used to befuddle the residents once they arrived. Aside from the fact that it was simply the moral thing to do, there was the possibility that they might lose any war with the Enemy. If they invaded, what chance would the residents of Paradise Towers stand of surviving if they were drugged into compliance with any orders they were given? No—they had to have their free will. It could well be the only thing that would give them any chance of survival.

But he was still scared stiff when he looked up into the framework he had to climb.

He could see a couple of the construction robots hard at work. They carried prefabricated wall and floor pieces up the dizzying ride without any fear, of course—they weren't programmed to know what fear was—but he was starting to feel sick as he watched them scurry about like huge, metallic insects. His legs were weak before he even began, and the robots danced about unconcerned.

Enough! The longer he stood here, the harder it would be to get his shaky legs into motion, and the easier it would become for him to flee back inside where it was safe—for him. He licked his dry lips, gathered together all of his courage, and began the next part of his climb. He released his hold on the upright and wiped his sweaty palms on his pants for the hundredth time. The only thing sustaining him against the relentless wind now was the terribly thin line anchoring him to the upright. And in a moment, he would have to reel this in…

From the apparatus on his back, he fired the twin grapples upwards. Not over the horizontal spar above him, but the one above that. He was shaking so much that he missed completely, and had to reel them back in. Once they were back in the mechanism, he aimed a little more carefully and fired again. The wind caught them, but they were heavy and firm enough, and though they shook a bit, they hit their target this time. He pulled on both ropes to make sure they were secure because his life literally depended on them holding. They seemed secure enough—but could he be sure?

He breathed in and out, on the verge of panicking. It had seemed—well, not easy, but at least conceivable—when he had planned this project. But now, here, standing in alternately blazing light and deep shadows… Now that his life was in the balance… His nerves were frayed raw.

Was it really worth it? Risking his life for a few thousand people he didn't even know? People he probably wouldn't even talk to or like if he met them in a social gathering? What did he really owe these unknown and unknowing folk? They wouldn't have a clue what he was risking on their behalf. And if he slipped, or if the wind grew stronger—strong enough to break these ropes—nobody would know, and he would have killed himself all for nothing. Were they worth such a risk? Wouldn't it be much, much better to give this insane idea up entirely and go back inside to safety?

He was almost ready to do this, until he knew what the consequences would be. Nobody would know that he was a coward… except himself. He'd be no better than the other sheep that had been placed on the Design Committee just to rubber-stamp anything their masters might decree. He'd be alive—but every day, every minute, he'd know that he'd abandoned his beliefs and failed the very people he was supposed to be supporting. He'd never be able to look into a mirror again without flinching from the sight of his cowardly countenance.

It would be better to be dead than to live like that.

Before he could have third-thoughts, he released the rope that held him firmly to the upright, and triggered the twin motors that raised him up the ropes over his head.

He almost screamed and peed his pants as the wind grabbed him and shook him as he ascended. His entire body shook with fear as he rose the ten feet or so to the next level. In panic, he threw his arms about the next upright. Then he realized that he hadn't cut the motors that were drawing him upwards and had to fumble with the switches to halt his ascent. It took all of his willpower to release one hand and use it to slowly attach his anchor rope and then free the grapples. He shook as they slide home in the mechanism on his shoulders.

He had managed the first floor of his ascent—and it had only almost terrified him to death. He had to stand, shaking, clasping the upright for dear life until he felt he could take control of his body again. And he had to do this again and again. He didn't think he would have the courage—but he couldn't go back without completing his self-appointed mission. Trembling, he took a deep breath and then lined up the grapples once again and fired.

The second ascent was less horrifying than the first Unfortunately, not by much. His heart was pounding crazily as he clutched the upright on the next floor and tried to reignite his will to do this for a third time. And then a fourth.

And then…

Somehow, he discovered that he was standing facing the Trank Tank. He couldn't even remember the last few ascents. His brain had simply frozen into repeating the same actions over and over again until he had gained his objective. He was breathing heavily, his heart still pounding away, his nerves fried. He was still high on the effects of the terror that shook his body. He was drenched in sweat, and his vision as well as his limbs was shaking. But he had made it! He was here, standing on a beam and staring at the object of his quest.

It didn't look like much—it had been designed to be hidden away, so there was no reason to spruce it up. It was simply a large box, twenty feet long, eight wide and three deep. The control access—of course!—was on the corner furthest from him. He could see bunches of pipes surrounding it and realized that it had already been hooked into the water supply for the entire building. Below the Tank, the floor (or ceiling) was partially constructed already, as were two of the walls that would hide it completely from view. He realized that if he'd delayed even a few days, it might have been impossible to get to it. His timing had somehow been almost perfect.

He had to force himself to start moving again. After the nerve-wracking ascent, walking along the horizontal beams was almost as calming as taking a summer walk in a park. But only comparatively, of course. He still had to fasten his safety line to the closest upright and then inch along the horizontal beam until he could clutch the next upright. But that was all; he'd judged his distances pretty well, all things considered. He was now only about ten feet from the tank. It would be a doddle!

Of course, he was deliberately not thinking about the fact that he'd have to reverse this terrifying trip to get back down to safety again… And, naturally, as soon as this thought occurred to him, he could think of nothing else.

No! he screamed mentally at himself. Think one step at a time! The task now was to replace the valve. Don't waste time and invite trouble by thinking of anything else. Especially not the trip back…

He was close enough now to grip the edge of the Tank. The two walls that had been constructed beyond it formed a kind of wind-break, and he had the flooring beneath his feet at last. No more perching on a horizon beam—he could just walk around the edge of the Tank.

He kept his safety line firmly attached, though—just in case.

Breathing more calmly, he walked around the Tank and to the access panel he needed. Finally, amazingly, he had reached his goal. Success was within reach now. But he had to be careful—he had to ensure that he left no traces that the Tank had been tampered with. He glanced at the panel, and saw that it had been closed using number 2 fasteners, as the plans had detailed. He reached in to the small pack he carried attached to his felt. Taking out the correct driver, he carefully unscrewed and stowed the fasteners. He couldn't afford to lose any of them—if he dropped even one, it would be noted in the next inspection and thus reveal his interference. Once the fasteners were out, he was able to slide the panel back to allow him access to the mechanism he had to replace.

In the glare of the construction lights, he could see reflections cast back at him.

The Trank Tank was already filled!

Were the drugs already circulating in the water supply system? It had never occurred to him that the plans for the sedatives had already been implemented. If the tranks were already moving throughout the building, would replacing the valve do anything at all? Or was he already too late to stop this insane scheme?

He fought down the panic he felt. No, at best only a very small portion of the drugs must have been deployed. If his valve was in place, it would prevent any further release. The small amount of drugs in the water would soon wear out, and not be replaced.

His plan could still work!

He had to lean over the Tank to get at the mechanism, but he prepared himself and –

'I have to admit,' said Liaison, 'you managed to make it further than I ever thought you would.'

In shock and terror, he jerked around.

One of the construction robots, spider-like, clung to an upright beside him, staring at him. There was a video screen in the 'face' of the mechanism, and on the screen was Liaison's grinning face.

He instinctively tried to back away, without recalling where he was and how badly off-balance.

His foot slipped, and he fell forward.

Into the Tank.

The Trank was chilled, and he screamed as he slapped into it. He stopped yelling and started choking and thrashing instead.

He felt really, really calm as he started drowning.

'How is he?' One Way asked, his voice carefully neutral.

'Perfectly fine,' Liaison replied. 'Fortunately, he'd had the foresight to tie himself to an upright. I had the robot grab the rope and pull him out.' He smiled. 'First time I've fished three thousand feet in the air.'

They were standing beside the bedside, looking down on the sleeping form of Jax. One Way had to admit that he did look very well for someone who'd almost drowned in a pool of tranks. 'You should have let him drown. It would have been better.'

'He might have given the drugs a funny taste.' Liaison shook his head 'Besides, you have to rather admire his courage and resourcefulness.' He glanced at the climbing harness that Jax had worn.

'He planned very well, and thought of ways to overcome all obstacles. He's just absolutely awful at concealing his intensions. He genuinely must have thought we wouldn't have anticipated his foolish actions.'

'You'll have even more trouble from him once he wakes,' One Way predicted. 'This isn't going to stop his misplaced idealism, you know.'

'On the contrary,' Liaison replied. 'It is.' He looked at the Committee Chairman. 'Do you have any idea how much trank he swallowed? Or was absorbed through his skin?' He shook his head. 'He's never going to question orders again, trust me. He will do precisely as he's told for the rest of his life.' He smiled down at the resting man. 'He'll still have all of his intelligence, of course, but it will be dedicated in whatever way we instruct him.'

One Way frowned. 'What do you have in mind? I assumed we would just fire him in disgrace. Do you intend to make a soldier of him?'

Liaison smiled—rather unpleasantly. 'He would make a good soldier, I agree,' he said. 'Obeying all orders without question… But, no. I think that would just be a waste, really. We already have thousands and thousands of unquestioning troops.' He reached down and patted Jax's shoulder. Even in his sleep, Jax smiled. 'No, I have a far better job in mind for him.

'I think we've just found the perfect Chief Caretaker—don't you?'

One Hundred and One Floors

Niki Haringsma

'—and the pleasure grotto's as opulent as ever,' Mr Hubart was saying. He lifted Mr Quisp's head, gently, and moved a wet flannel over the blotched wrinkles. It was as far down as Mr Quisp could still feel anything. Everything below the neck was numb meat. 'That's still the highlight of 100, it is. They've formed a little string quartet down there, Mindy and that sister of hers, and the lovely couple in the apartment just across, remember? They do Schubert.' He patted the pale cheeks dry. 'All clean.'

'You're such a dear.' Mr Quisp smiled like a well-groomed cat.

'Well.' Mr Hubart licked his lips nervously. 'Shall we finally… do it?'

'Not tonight, darling,' Mr Quisp said with a sigh. 'I'm ever so tired.'

Mr Hubart was quiet a moment. 'You wouldn't feel—'

'Come back tomorrow, my boy. And tell me one more gorgeous lie.' He yawned. 'We'll be up to floor 101, won't we? Now, you tell me all about their grand parties, and their scandals, and what ghastly shawls Mrs Ducomble wears these days.'

Mr Hubart eyed Mr Quisp's plump fingers. 'And *then* you'll let me have a taste? Just a little one?'

'Of course,' Mr Quisp said, already dozing off. 'Pinky promise.'

The Queen in Yellow

Ian Potter

It'd been Disposal Chute who found the brochure. She'd been on outlook on floor 78, watching the robot Cleaners and Caretakers at work on a carrydoor off Sulphate Street. A condemned flat was getting deep scrubbed for renovation, the last one of its row.

A pair of disgruntled Caretakers in masks and goggles and heavy gauntlets were piling robot waste trucks high with old brickletat—dusty scraps of a life, long overgrown with mould. Judging by the furnishings being disposed of, the flat had belonged to a very old Rezzie. There was a tiny vidbox, a battered, worn armchair, long collapsed in its middle, with a little white cloth on like you saw on hiss-tree discs, dozens of ceramic nack-nicks—doe-eyed shepherdesses, smiling beggar boys, timid woodland creatures, and mounds of ancient paper mags. There wasn't much for the Yellow Kangs in that haul, even if the mags were yellowed.

Although she couldn't read their faces for their masks and eye protectors, Disposal Chute could tell the Caretakers were repulsed by their work. Their foreheads were creased like old linen and sweat-shiny from their work. One constantly sprayed Bugzap. The other spoke almost entirely in grunts and swearwords, as he loaded a Cleaner's storage bin with fresh heaps of detritus.

'S'no good for my scallard back, this! Why can't we fit these claw clanks with proper arms for this feek?'

The Caretaker with the fly spray just shrugged.

'Handling this cank's well above my paygrade,' the other continued, indicating a faded, threadbare footstool with a discoloured top cushion. 'I mean this grubber's wet! Soaked through with milgak! Can't be good for my lungs.' He heaved another pile of browned and stained keepsakes into a truck, seeming not to notice the watchy disc that slipped between his gauntlets as he tipped it all inside.

The disc fell to the carrydoor floor, its impact masked by a crash of tiny china figurines. It bounced, spun and rolled into a cobwebbed corner where it wobbled to a halt.

'I'm going to memo the flinking San committee—we need better clanking robots.'

There had been a lot of 'renovations' in the 70s recently, particularly on West side. All they ever seemed to amount to was chipboard being staple-nailed to a door, and yellow and black warning tape being festooned across a carrydoor. It had been the tape that made Disposal Chute linger. That stuff was a gift for the Kangs and Disposal Chute had a particular Kang in mind.

Once the impassive cleaning machines and ill-tempered men had moved on, Disposal Chute emerged from her hidey duct to claim-bag her spoils and tag the scene. She balled up the Cleaners' warning tape streamers and wrenched a handful of staple-nails from the board over the condemned flat's door. She could make bosscrow bolts from those. Once she'd removed the loosest she set to work with her paint sprays.

Wallscrawling on chipboard wasn't as much fun as on walls, the surface was porous and the paint didn't apply well, but any territory the Yellows could stake a claim to mattered in the Kang Game. Particularly now.

In the middle of the chipboard was a Caretakers' notice—a single sheet of paper sticky-mounted in place.

CLOSED FOR RENOVATIONS.
NEW DEVELOPMENTS COMING.
WATCH FOR IMPROVEMENT.
BUILD HIGH FOR HAPPINESS.

In smaller letters below was appended:

Unauthorised egress is a criminal offence and against building regulations.

Below that, in smaller letters still, were three dense lines of text, a mass of jargon, dashes, parentheses and numbers, all followed up by the Chief Caretaker's stamp.

Disposal Chute took her small details nozzle-can from her belt-sac, rattled it in staccato Yellow Kang rhythm and sprayed an addendum to the notice in Vivid Day-Glo SunshineTM.

NO FLYPOSTS!

Then she got working on a stencil-tag, sticky-tacking the template to the wall marked for spraying.

It was only when she'd finished her handiwork, and finally turned to leave, that she'd spotted the fallen watchy disc. It glinted from the shadows like rat eyes caught in the beam of a flashlamp. She footed over to eggsham it. The disc didn't seem scarred or tarnished, so there was a hopechance it might play.

It wasn't likely to hold any icehot vids but it would at least be new. The Yellow Kangs didn't have much viewing now—a few salvaged toons, an entertainment about a thing called a motel (an impossibly glamorous relic from the days before), and a strange weepy-watchy set on a world without colours where in-betweens kept singing not talking.

They reckoned that one must have come from a time before the war—there was much outgoing in it.

Disposal Chute took the watchy disc to a Picturespout on Argon Street, carefully selecting a route that kept to camera blind spots. It was one of the public players you could run off the lighting circuit without the Caretakers spotting spikes, but you had to be briskful. She spooled through the disc at tenspeed, not expecting much. It was some sort of promotional presentation from the Towers' early days and she'd almost decided the thing was only fit to refabshion as a throwblade when she caught sight of the treasure. Outtaking the disc, she talkiphoned Brainquarters and footed hurriedly to base.

The Yellow Kangs' new Brainquarters, the adapted space they'd made their Hide-In, was up on floor 92, or, strictly speaking, beneath it. Floor 92 had been one of the levels with a fountain square when Paradise Towers first opened, but the water had soon greened with algae and the fountain mechanism become unreliable. After, a few increasingly token, repair jobs, the pump had been quietly turned off. The forgotten underfloor tank below the dried up water feature wasn't as near to working washrooms as the Kangs might have liked, but it was an icehot place to sleep and stash supplies. Most important of all, its unobtrusive entrance hatch was easy to defend, even with small numbers.

Disposal Chute crouched down and rapped at the floor hatch in the same rhythm she'd rattled her nozzle-can before. Passwords were exchanged. 'Build High For Happiness!', 'Custard over cutlets!' and the panel was opened from within.

Inside the metal tank crouched her fellow Kangs—Emergency Light, Do Not Cross and Key Card. Key Card upright on her beanbed, Emergency Light had squeezed into a corner between the coldbox and ping-oven and Do Not Cross held up the hatch panel in her strong brown hands. Disposal Chute slid down to join them, her fingers brushing against Do Not Cross's as they repositioned the hatch behind her.

It was surprisingly bright inside the tank. Do Not Cross had found some old metal polish on a paint raid that gave a slight sheen to the rusty old walls and helped reflect back the fairy lights they'd hung about their Hide-In, bathing the space in a warm yellow light.

The Kangs exchanged their traditional how you dos and hails with pat-a-cake and hand-jive gestures now deeply engrained, then Key Card shifted herself on her long beany throne. The polystyrene beads within it stirred as she moved, hissing like the static on a Caretaker's LCDE.

'So, what you find, Disposal Chute?' she asked flatly. 'What was so icehot you couldn't speak it on talkiphone?'

'Gold!' replied Disposal Chute, letting balled up yellow and black warning tape unroll from her hand. It bounced down in coils like springy plastic ringlets. She smiled at Do Not Cross. 'It's got your name on it,' she said. 'I thought I could ribbon up your hair.' Do Not Cross grinned back.

'High Fabshion!' scowled Key Card. 'Is that all? I'd hoped for food.'

Everyone was hungry in Paradise Towers. Some nights, Key Card felt like you could hear the hunger throbbing through the building—the Towers' gurgling plumbing echoing the churn of empty bellies. The Rezzies at least had meals on wheels once a quarter, or were supposed to anyway, and there was some talk that the Caretakers had window box allotments.

It was much harder for the Kangs. Most of the vending machines didn't get filled anymore. The Kangs weren't entirely sure the few new snacks there were, were really all that new. There were no eat by dates on any of them.

If they could get hold of nicosticks, they kept the pangs at bay, but there wasn't much left in the Yellow Kang coldbox—a few readychows, a potfoodle and a tray of sticky-tack with ice in. If you could bag a rat with your arrowgun you at least knew that was fresh.

'I am grateful, Disposal Chute,' said Do Not Cross quietly. She would be, thought Key Card.

'I carry more than treasure for you,' Disposal Chute continued, 'I've High Fabshion for us all!' She pulled the new watchy disc from her ragged yellow strap-pouch and placed it in the Brainquarters' vidbox. The whole tank lit up with the glow of its screen.

'What's this one?' asked Emergency Light. 'Another roman-tick?'

There were often roman-tick discs in Oldsters' vid collections. They usually featured kissing, young in-between women and men old enough to be Caretakers. Emergency Light didn't like roman-ticks at all. They made her feel sick in her tummy, rat-rissole sick.

Disposal Chute spooled the disc forward.

Images of Paradise Towers filled the vidbox, but not the Towers as they were now, with broken windows and flickering lightballs. The Towers on screen were clean, new and shining, stripped of weeds and crumbled concrete.

'Oh, yawny,' said Key Card, 'hiss-tree.'

'It's just an old Rezzies' welcome pack,' said Emergency Light. This was probably worse than kissing.

'Yeah, a comewell brochure, but wait, it gets undull.'

The gleaming streets and squares of Paradise Towers sped by on the screen, happy residents raced through them like insects fleeing sprinkle gas and Bugzap, then, as the camera entered an apartment, Disposal Chute slowed the picture to a quarterspeed crawl.

The camera lingered on an airy, open living space—sunlight streaming in through tall sparkling windows.

'Look!'

'What?'

Emergency Light didn't notice waystraight, but Do Not Cross did.

'Yellow curtains,' she breathed.

Billowing slightly in the slow-motion breeze from the windows were heavy mustard velvet drapes—thick, pleated and brocaded, gathered with silky yellow rope tiebacks that held the pleats in place.

'This is from floor 78, West Side,' said Disposal Chute. 'Wall side apartments. All the furnishings are yellow.'

'Soand?' said Key Card.

Everyone knew the floors of Paradise Towers had been colour coded in the early days. That was how Kang fabshions had begun at time start, back when Kangs lived in flats.

'So, the Caretakers just unopened a whole carrydoor on 78 West Side! 1974 off Sulphate Street. A carrydoor that's probably never been redecked or raided. There'll be more yellow cloth in those flats than we've seen in yearlongs. No Blue Kangs burning it as Judies, no Rezzies guarding, Caretakers all where-else. All just upboarded and waiting. Think what gearments we could make!'

The Yellow Kangs' clothes weren't what they had been. Grubby from old Carob-yums and stained with sticky Fizzade, they'd been patched and mended so often, most were more stitching than fabric. The Yellow Kang Brainquarters had once boasted garbrobes chockfull with bright yellow, but that had been back in the Grotto of Contentment, before Air Vent had betrayed them to the Reds.

The signs had been there a while, but if you were young and past naming in Paradise Towers, the last thing you did was pay signs any heed. Signs stopped you having fun.

Air Vent had got hold of some sheets for dyeing from an abandoned floor's laundrette, but something had gone wrong while she'd been treating them in the washroom and they'd somehow outcome all orange. The Kangs had let it pass. They'd even let Air Vent wear the tunics and scarves she cut from the orange linen. Allafter, they were far more yellow than not so—golden in a way that picked out Air Vent's long blonde hair. Even when her roots started going russet, no one questioned. The Kangs knew bleach could be hard to score and the colour suited her pale skin.

Then one day Air Vent was gone, fallen to the Red Kangs, and she'd taken Sanitary Disposal and half their garbrobe with her.

Even now the Yellow Kangs still caught sight of Red Kangs on the Eye-Spies, striding proudly through their tag zones in red-stained garments that they knew had once been theirs.

'All Kangs are on down-me-hands now,' said Disposal Chute. 'Mends and make-dos—borrows and steals, but if we make new fabshions, we can make new Kangs! The Reds and Blues will give up their drab-rags and join Yellow Kangs in multipack!'

'Don't want no green and orange,' Key Card truculently replied. 'We should stay pure Yellow.'

'Pure Yellow and four,' Disposal Chute sighed, 'if we don't recruit new Yellow Kangs, we lose the few tag zones we still have.'

'Cutlet words,' scoffed Key Card.

Key Card had never liked Disposal Chute. It wasn't that Disposal Chute threatened her leadership and it certainly wasn't because of her friendship with Do Not Cross. Key Card had nothing to be jealous of there. She was leader—she could have all the friends she wanted. The problem was Disposal Chute was new and still didn't quite fit in. Obviously, they'd welcomed her open-arms and with full pat-a-cake and hand jive when she'd asked to join. Any new Yellow Kang was to be embraced now the Blues and Reds were gaining floors, and Disposal Chute had acquitted herself well during the Siege of Twilight Square and the Neon Footway Turnabout, but, after months as a Yellow, she was still an outsider. She'd grown up on one of the upper floors on the other side of the Towers, and spoke in a high North Two Hundreds accent. There were odd bits of slang that made her seem alien or babyish—'bosscrow' for arrow gun or 'delish' for unvom, things no proper Kang would say. The worst of it was Key Card had noticed the other Kangs starting to copycat. It wasn't just Do Not Cross giggling at Disposal Chute's funny upfloor ways, Key Card had even caught Emergency Lighting calling rat-chewed wires 'rodentured'. The Kangs were speaking more of themselves and less of the tribe now, even Key Card herself, if uncareful. They were outtrying unworn phrases—using strange new words with new ideas attached, words that brought disagreement.

They were asking questions, having thoughts that made the group weaker.

'Ware, Key Card,' said Disposal Chute. 'I'm no Cutlet!'

It was no way to talk to a leader

'And can you show purchase-proof?' Key Card rejoined.

'Oh, safe-style!' Disposal Chute answered, in that mannered little 'good-child' voice that made her sound a rezzie-pleaser. 'I'm going to raid that carrydoor and bring back the yellow!'

Key Card blanched.

'So, who's with me?' Disposal Chute continued.

Do Not Cross's arm shot up at once, striking the tank ceiling hard so it rang like a bell. Emergency Lighting's hand hovered near her chin as she glanced across to her leader.

'Too risky for all go,' said Key Card quickly, seizing the initiative. 'Onesome must guard the Brainquarters 'gainst Kang-raid or Caretaking.'

'Can you manage alone?' asked Emergency Lighting gently, finally committing to raising her hand.

'No to-do,' said Key Card. 'That's why I'm leader.' Things hadn't gone quite as she'd hoped.

It was decided a night raid would be safest. Caretaker patrols were less regular after curfew and, now Disposal Chute had tagged it, word would have spread by talkiphone and Eye-Spy that 78 West was a Yellow held zone. There was little chance of other Kangs attempting claimback 'til they'd fully checked it for snares, and they'd not dare try that in lights down. Key Card graciously awarded her three scouts a prized sharebag of Crunchsnak and carefully presented them with three ice tokens from the coldbox. The thin discs of ice had been carefully pressed into the shape of token coins, or rather the one real one the Kangs possessed, in their sticky-tack mould.

'For Fizzade,' Key Card explained. They'd found out a long time ago the Towers' soft drinks dispensers would take anything shaped like a token coin if it was roughly the right weight. 'If the flat plumbing's offturned, you don't want to go thirsty.'

Her followers nodded solemnly, accepting her gifts.

'Best move before these Kroggs melt and get them to a Drinksmat,' said Disposal Chute.

'But what if we can't find unbroke Drinksmats?' Emergency Light asked.

'We drink the tokens!' said Do Not Cross brightly.

Emergency Light and Disposal Chute both laughed, much more than was necessary in Key Card's opinion.

'Ware how you use them,' Key Card added as they left. 'Be safe-sure you're unwatched. Other Kangs don't know how to work Drinksmats yet.'

The others nodded. 'Yellow Kangs are best!' they chorused, stamping their feet to the Yellow Kang beat as they headed from the Square. 'Yellow Kangs are best!'

Knowing how to get soft drinks was probably the only arena in which their boast still held true.

The easiest way for the Kangs to get down to floor 78 would have been to take the stairs, the alleviators were too much of a lotto-bet. Unfortunately, the lower hundred stairways were closely monitored with cameras that might draw attention to their raid. They also tended to get very wet and sometimes smelly. Some higher level Oldsters didn't much like their downstairs neighbours and they had buckets, diuretics and Gravity on their side...

The simplest path avoiding detection or a soaking was through the ventilation system, but the Towers' ventilation shafts weren't half as easy to crawl through as the ones on old watchy discs. The Kangs assumed designs had moved on, perhaps thanks to Kroagnon, the Towers' famed Great Architect. The shafts were cramped and thick with cobwebs and coated in a strange sticky fur-—presumably, something formed from layers of damp dust and stray hair. And even though the ducting layout seemed straightforward, there were still occasional internal fans to detach and unexpected support struts to negotiate with stray sharp edges that made progress through the system hard.

Once everyone had scored Fizzade, it was decided Emergency Lighting should lead the way through the shafts. She was the broadest, Disposal Chute explained. Any route she could pass through the others could follow safe-style.

Emergency Lighting wished Disposal Chute could have left that unsaid. She didn't always think this new Kang liked her, and as Emergency Lighting squeezed into the cramped pipeway she thought she heard her and Do Not Cross giggle behind her. 'Not her first time inside an air vent!' she imagined Disposal Chute was whispering. She was probably mistaken. It was hard to hear inside the tight crawl. Her fellows were probably just discussing the size of her backside or the dangers of crawling behind it.

The joke wouldn't have been fair anyway, she'd not been friends with Air Vent at all. She'd not known anyone like that since Wet Floor on Judy Night.

Carrying the coiled rope that the Kangs would use to drop fourteen floors, Emergency Lighting pulled herself through the ducting, lighting the way ahead with a flashlamp strapped to her forehead. The pounding gurgle of the Towers' pipes in the enclosed metallic space filled her ears. It was like the swishing medscan heartbeat of a gigantic angry beast. As she negotiated a tight turning at a T-joint corner, Emergency Lighting flinched involuntarily as her face broke through a dusty cobweb film. Something scuttled across her hand and scurried off into the dark. It felt big.

'Ach!' she wailed. 'Why would spiders want to live all the way down here?'

'Because flies and bugglets do,' said Disposal Chute behind her.

'Nothot,' said Emergency Lighting grimly.

'Brave and bold, brave and bold,' Do Not Cross called forward, gently reminding Emergency Lighting of the true Kang way.

'Easy for the back Kang to say!' Emergency Lighting replied. 'I squish all the bugglets for you!'

'Don't be a grizzle,' Disposal Chute sighed, 'there aren't that many bugglets.'

'The spiders will have eaten most of them,' Do Not Cross added unhelpfully.

Emergency Lighting crawled on.

'How big do you think spiders get in here?' she asked, as she shuffled forward 'round the bend.

'Bout so big.'

Do Not Cross did something with her hands.

'I'm in front of you! I can't see that!'

'Big enough for rats to eat,' said Disposal Chute. 'Not so big they eat rats.'

Emergency Lighting allowed herself a hollow chuckle until Disposal Chute added an uncertain 'mayhaps'.

It took almost half an hour to get to the drop junction, and about the same again to descend the down shaft in stages to reach floor 78. There was an unpleasant pulsing updraft all the time they descended. It was accompanied by the rough wheezing of huge pumps far below, pushing hot air 'round the building-—smelly, warm breath with a perturbing rattle, like Key Card snoring after ethanolop but a hundred times louder.

When the Kangs finally emerged into the carrydoor on floor 78, the knees of their yellow leggings were snagged and thick with dirt and Emergency Lighting's undertunic was nearly worn through at the elbows. They cleared their throats with warm Fizzade and stretched their arms and legs, eagerly relishing their freedom.

'Is this the right junction?'

Disposal Chute angled Emergency Lighting's head up so her flashlamp beam picked out the carrydoor code. 078/1974/223 was emblazoned at the wall top by an arrow sign for Sulphate Street.

'I never forget a vent path,' said Disposal Chute archly. She'd never sounded more top floors. 'Anyway,' she continued with ill-disguised pride, 'that's a big clue.' She nodded to the wallscrawl further down the wall.

On a chipboard panel to their left was scrawled the slogan 'Yellow Kangs are best!' Lower down the panel 'No Flyposts!' had been sprayed over a Caretakers' notice. To the right of the panel was a crudely stencilled picture, in dribbling red, blue and black. It depicted two Kangs, each holding the hand of a Caretaker who stood between them.

Disposal Chute was clearly pleased with this one. She loved needling the opposition and this was classic Gameskangship.

'Icehot, eh?'

Bit banksy, thought Emergency Lighting. It was a long-ago phrase for scrawls that were slightly underwhelming or obvious. She didn't quite know where it came from but knew it was a phrase it was better not to say out loud.

Quietly, the three Kangs set to work removing the chipboard panel to expose the condemned flat's door. It came away quite easily, Disposal Chute had already taken most of the staple-nails that secured it in place.

The door behind the panel was a sturdy one, one of the original Towers doors—thick and solid and grown of actual vat wood.

'Here since time start!' Do Not Cross whistled appreciatively. 'No substitutions!'

Most flat doors had been replaced at least once by now for one reason or another, and the new ones couldn't hold a glo-stick to the originals. They were flimsy things you could break with ridiculous ease if you knew their structural weak points, which meant a lot of the replacements had been replaced themselves in turn. Door crashing was a good way to annoy Caretakers or keep them out of a game zone while they got out their carpentry tools. This original door looked a bit solid for that.

Emergency Lighting tried to break the door anyway, 'I am heaviest,' she said with an edge the others didn't detect, and ran at it hard. She'd learned the door crashing knack from floor 109's gun-nut, though no one was supposed to know that. You had to keep your distance from the Musclebrain in case he had thoughts. He watched roman-tick discs too and was much younger than the Rezzies.

The door didn't give and Emergency Lighting bounced straight off it. As she toppled back, Do Not Cross made a noise that might have been clearing ventilation dust from her throat. It was impossible to be sure and would be pointless to challenge.

'No give-budge,' said Emergency Lighting weakly.

The Kangs eggshammed the few precious knives they'd brought with them—rat-gutters and wire-cutters, not fit for much tougher. If they were going to get into the flat, they'd need to gouge a hole through the door until they could spring the lock open. They began chipping away carefully, trying not to blunt their prized tools, working in shifts until they finally got through.

Deftly, Do Not Cross twing-snipped the mechanism, and the door swung open.

The first thing the Kangs noticed as they stepped into the darkened flat was the smell—initially quite delicious and then slightly offputting—fly-spray and carpetfresh, but with something sweet beneath.

'What's the scent?' Emergency Lighting asked. Her voice echoed hard in a room clearly stripped of soft furnishing. 'Is that dessert-whip?'

'I don't think so.'

Do Not Cross's flashlamp picked out a mesh of fine strands glittering in the gloom 'Emergency Lighting! More cobwebs for you!'

Emergency Lighting made a point of striding bravely forward. 'Why's the floor crunchy?'

'Sprinkle gas residue. Dead bugglets,' Disposal Chute answered. 'The Cleaners went deep-clean.

'Tough on the spiders,' said Do Not Cross as she followed. She halted, her ears picking up a familiar sound in the dark. 'Something's buzzing over here.'

'Mayhaps angry flies.'

Do Not Cross strode across the room, moving her head from side to side, trying to locate the sound's source.

Disposal Chute turned a wall dial and the apartment's lights flickered on. The flat was shockingly bare. There were deep dents in the carpet where furniture had once been and dark rectangles on the faded candy-stripe wallpaper where pictures had once hung, but there wasn't a great deal more.

'Lights work,' said Disposal Chute, 'I thought they'd have downpowered the electricals.'

The Kangs took off their flashlamps in relief. The mounting straps had cut in painfully by their ears. Do Not Cross laughed out loud at the dirty tidemark the flashlamp had left on Emergency Lighting's face.

Emergency Lighting ignored her. 'Disposal Chute,' she asked, 'why haven't they offcut the circuit?'

Disposal Chute just shrugged.

Do Not Cross was standing by a breakfast bar in the corner of the room's open plan kitchen. She'd located her buzzing. 'Maybe because they left the coldbox on?' she said. The kitchen coldbox was tall, clearly much bigger than the one at Brainquarters.

'They took the curtains,' said Emergency Lighting flatly.

Disposal Chute's face fell. 'Ah, blank walls and Cleaners! I didn't see any outcoming!'

It was true though. All the room's windows were bare.

'Maybe the Rezzie downtook them?' Do Not Cross suggested. 'They wouldn't have been needed.' She pointed out through the condensation fogged panes. There was nothing at all to see, not even a star or hint of fog bank glowing from the towers' lights. The windows were thick with ivy. Dark green leaved creepers covered them entirely, sticking fast to the plasglass on pale gummy rootlets, a mass of tiny white tubes that looked like sickly bugglets. Day or night, the dense foliage outside would have made curtains superfluous.

Emergency Lighting wandered away to check a side room, as Disposal Chute joined Do Not Cross by the coldbox. 'There's a bed in here,' Emergency Lighting called back, 'and a little washroom too!'

'Check if it's unplumbed,' Do Not Cross shouted through, and a few moments later she and Disposal Chute heard the chugging, air-locked pipes begin to glug and water run clear. 'Oh, but this is icehot!' Emergency Lighting announced, gleefully flushing the laviflow.

'Water on too,' Disposal Chute mused. 'Looks like Caretakers are planning on relocation.'

'Why, who needs new flats? We're getting fewer, not more.'

'Mayhaps the Towers are getting new Rezzies.'

'Where from?' asked Do Not Cross.

'I don't know. The war?'

'You think it's over?'

'Not sure. Mayhaps. Might be getting injured fighters back. Might be getting victors.'

'The in-betweens?'

'If it's in-betweens who's won.'

Strange creaks started to emerge from the adjoining room. Emergency Lighting was laughing. 'Oh my safe days! This bed! It's unlumpy. It's all spring-shaped!'

'Good?' Do Not Cross inquired.

'No, too unsoft,' Emergency Lighting replied. There was a brief pause. 'I could get used to it though.'

Do Not Cross grinned and shook her golden locks, the freshly braided warning tape rustled as she did.

Disposal Chute had opened the huge coldbox. Inside, it was crammed with boxed up food. 'I think meals on wheels have been.'

The coldbox's contents could have fed a queen, particularly one keen on carobtort and soy-style vol-au-ventlets. Ready meals were stacked high on every shelf, all with readable use by dates and apparently unopened.

Disposal Chute checked the packets in amazement. 'Some of these are good for months still.'

Emergency Lighting came up behind her, her face now wet and clean. 'I don't think I've eaten cake that was meant for the future before,' she said slowly.

'Before?' Do Not Cross queried.

The three Kangs shared a look. They were all raging with hunger, far more than a Crunchsnak sharebag would assuage.

Do Not Cross pulled a carton of limonizzle cake from the coldbox. The packaging fell open surprisingly easy. 'This one should be consumed next year!'

'I almost want to wait 'til it's ready,' Emergency Lighting said.

'Almost,' laughed Disposal Chute.

'Do you think we should we try a bit?'

'I think we should try it all,' said Disposal Chute emboldened, scooping a chunk of cake out with her fingers. It was chilled not iced, so there was no need to oven-ping it.

The cake was full-flavoured, rich and creamy and almost too sweet to bear, yet somehow the three Kangs battled through, their hands quickly thick with fondant icing and, almost as quickly, licked clean.

Eventually, when the cake was little more than crumbs and a smear of yellow on open cardboard, Emergency Lighting spoke.

'We should take some back to Key Card.' Key Card wouldn't miss the unfound curtains if they brought back food to replace it.

Disposal Chute shook her head. 'Through the ventilation shafts? We'd crush it. It'd get hot in all the updraft.'

'She'd do better to come here,' Do Not Cross suggested.

'But Key Card won't leave the Brainquarters unguarded,' Emergency Lighting protested, 'not after last time.'

'If we declare this our new Kang base, she won't need to,' said Disposal Chute.

'We can't just move our Hide-In!' Emergency Lighting was shocked. The Kang Game had rules.

'Can't we?' Do Not Cross enquired. 'We did when the Reds found our Grotto.'

Emergency Lighting felt uneasy. The idea felt unloyal. 'But not without say-so! Key Card should decide!'

'When Key Card sees the flat, she'll have to agree. She'll want that bed of yours for first-off.'

Emergency Lighting flushed slightly. 'It's not mine!' she began. 'And Kangs belong on the streets not inwith flats!'

'Says who? We were all in flats at time start. All the first Kangs kept their flats in the new days—Registered Assembly Point, Loose Tiling, High Voltage, No Petting…' It was a litany of the greats, the founding Kangs who'd been teenagers when they'd just been little girls. The first players who'd upmade the Game's rules.

'Brainquarters are best,' said Emergency Lighting firmly.

'And why can't a flat be a Brainquarters?' said Do Not Cross. 'This place is icehot! Better than neath the fountain.'

'Look,' said Disposal Chute waving at a gadget on the kitchen surface, 'electrical blade sharp. Could make a bosscrow bolt prick-pinned, like that!' She clicked her fingers.

'My arrows are sharp already,' Emergency Lighting replied, tacitly choosing sides with her choice of language.

'And your throwblades? This could hone an edge-side haste-pace! Slice through plas-cans! Snick through rats…'

'This is not a Brainquarters,' Emergency Lighting snapped back.

'What don't you like here?' Do Not Cross teased. 'It's not the cobwebs, is it?' She pulled a tangled strand from the wall to wave in Emergency Lighting's face. Then she stopped.

'Disposal Chute! This isn't cobweb… This is yellow…' The third Kang came closer, eggshamming the fine fibres in Do Not Cross's hand, rolling them between her fingers. She felt the delicate yellow filaments stretch and fray beneath her touch. Do Not Cross was right, it definitely wasn't cobweb.

'Nagged snylon,' Disposal Chute concluded. 'Synthetic.'

'From the curtains?'

'Where eggshact did you get this?' Disposal Chute demanded.

Do Not Cross indicated the clump of snagged fibres somehow caught on the wall, a few strands slowly twisting in an air-conditioned draught. The threads had been trapped in a thin crack that none of the Kangs had noticed—a vertical straight line they'd read as part of the wallpaper design. Disposal Chute rapped the wall lightly, in Yellow Kang time from complete force of habit. It sounded hollow, thin. 'Dial off the light,' she said, her voice so urgent that Emergency Lighting did so without question.

The room plunged back into darkness. Emergency Lighting fumbled for her flashlamp.

'No.'

'What then?'

'Wait.'

The Kangs stood in silence in the gloom, listening to the quiet gurgle of the Towers' pipes, the rhythmic hiss of its air, the buzz of the coldbox and their own excited heartbeats, set racing with sugar and discovery.

'I can hear another sound,' Do Not Cross whispered. 'Squeak bleeps, unregular.'

The others strained their ears until they too could detect it—a faint irregular chirrup somewhere in the dark. It was high-pitched and burbling with occasional unexpected trills—like the sounds from some old handgame chockfull of jumping and collecting.

'I think it's coming from next door.'

Slowly, as the Kangs listened and their eyes adjusted to the shadows, they began to make out a faint glow in the blackness. Through the crack in the wall shone a blade-thin slice of light.

'I think I know where our curtains went,' Disposal Chute said.

The Kangs knives were too thick to prise the narrow wall crack open and even with throwblade discs buffed thin by the electrical sharpener, it took about ten minutes to force the concealed door open sufficiently to locate the hidden latch within. The Kangs felt clumsy in their work now, hot and tired from their exertions despite the flat's heating not being on, but once they'd eventually found the latch it took just seconds to outspring.

The wallpaper covered door enticingly creaked open. The Kangs stepped through into a dimly lit room and the door swung back hard behind them, clunking firmly shut.

'Sprung closer,' said Disposal Chute as her eyes adjusted to the light. The room seemed to be suffused in dim amber, like the light from a cot bulb she half remembered long ago. She tried to blot out the sounds the memory brought to mind. Sad times and cruel voices.

Forcing her mind back to the herenow, Disposal Chute stumbled through to where the light controller should be. The floor felt different in this flat, but the room seemed to have roughly the same outlay as the one they'd just left. After fumbling about for a minute for the control, she managed to turn up the dimmer to see the flat clearly. It was virtually identical to the one they'd just left, but even more bare— no coldbox, no curtains, no carpet, nothing but a tiny ornate cage that swung from the ceiling, slowly turning in the air. Inside it was a small yellow bird, the source of the high-pitched squeaking. As the light levels rose, its calls became more animated and it began rapping a tiny mirror and shaking its cage bars.

'A cannery!' said Do Not Cross.

'Where you make cans?' Emergency Lighting asked, blinking in the light.

'No, the other kind of cannery. The kind that makes canneries.'

Emergency Lighting was still puzzled.

'It's a bird,' said Disposal Chute, 'a pet.'

'No Petting!' a strange voice seemed to whisper from the walls. It made Do Not Cross jump but no one else seemed to hear it. It must just have been air, trapped, bubbling in the plumbing.

'It's so yellow!' said Emergency Lighting in awe. The brightness of the bird was almost painful to look at and it seemed to keep slipping out of focus as the cage rotated on its chain.

Disposal Chute watched too, staring at the bird, enraptured as it sipped water from its bottle and took a tiny nibble of seed. 'If we can't find any curtains, we can always take this thing back to Key Card.'

'Neath the fountain? Too noisy,' said Do Not Cross. The bird's song was already slightly painful. She didn't like to imagine that shrill call echoing through the water tank.

'Not if it was unalive,' Disposal Chute suggested. 'Might taste good. We could oven ping it and fabshion headgarbs from the feathers.'

She distractedly stroked the strips of warning tape woven into Do Not Cross's hair. Do Not Cross sniggered.

Emergency Lighting didn't like this. 'No! Kangs don't kill, Disposal Chute! No wipe-outs! It's a rule.'

'Calm down, Caretaker!' Do Not Cross snapped back cruelly.

'No. We don't make things unalive!'

'Except for rats and accidents,' Disposal Chute suggested, 'and the poor little bugglets that we squish beneath our bellies…'

Emergency Lighting felt her face redden, suddenly very hot—like the flames of a Judy Night effigy burning an arm's length away, like that night Wet Floor took her hand as they torched stolen Blue Kang clothing and waited for the sprinklers to kick in. She felt sick and confused and rushed to the side room she hoped contained a laviflow.

Do Not Cross watched Disposal Chute, she seemed mesmerised by the bird cage's movement. Something was bothering her somehow.

'Why are these rooms joined, Disposal Chute?'

'Mayhaps the old Rezzie was a Do-It-Yourselfer. Throughknocked to her neighbour.'

'Why?'

'Mayhaps they were lovers and didn't want the other Rezzies to know.' She gave Do Not Cross a look that could have set a hundred fountains dancing. 'It can happen.'

'Yes, but…' Do Not Cross struggled to find the words to express eggshactly what felt odd.

From the adjoining room they heard retching and the flush of the laviflow. They started laughing out loud, as if this was the funniest thing ever.

'Best help,' said Do Not Cross eventually and, bent double, still chuckling, the friends headed to the bedroom. Emergency Lighting was lying in there, sprawled across the bed, restlessly turning on the mattress.

'You alright?' asked Do Not Cross.

'No,' said Emergency Lighting.

'What matter?'

'Belly not right. This bed too soft now.'

'Not like Key Card's beanbed?' Disposal Chute found herself saying.

Do Not Cross struggled with a thought. None of this was good. None of them were acting sound-style. She turned to Disposal Chute and struggled to focus on her face. It didn't quite seem to be her.

'Disposal Chute! Something's gone unright!' she screamed. Her friend's swimming features seemed to snap back into focus as she turned to face her in confusion.

'What?'

'The cannery…' Do Not Cross began, then the thought that she'd been hunting suddenly fell into place. 'It has fresh water, a full seed dispenser! Onesome's living here!'

Disposal Chute looked puzzled. 'Why make all like this?'

She heard a sound, perhaps in the walls, or perhaps her pulse pound in her head. Scuttling like a huge spider… in Yellow Kang rhythm.

'I think we're in a trap! Come on!' She turned to go.

'But Emergency Lighting?' Do Not Cross managed to protest.

'She ate more cake. She's too heavy to carry.' The thought somehow made some sense.

Holding each other upright, the friends staggered from the bedroom into the body of the flat.

'Need to get out!' Disposal Chute lurched to the concealed door and tried to reopen it. Her fingers felt fat and unhelpful and couldn't find the edge. All the time the cannery was screeching, harsh and distressing like fingers scraping down plasglass.

'Can't open!'

'I'll try the front door!' slurred Do Not Cross as she half fell towards it. It was as solid and heavy as the one they'd broken through and it seemed to be locked fast.

Disposal Chute fumbled in her belt-sac for a throwblade she could slide into the hidden door crack, but her eager, clumsy hands grabbed at it too hard. As she pulled it free from its carry case it seemed to leave a trail behind it—a bright arc of scarlet streamers falling in halftime through the air.

'Red Kangs!' she gasped as she slumped back against the wall. Everything seemed to be falling away now—the flat lights fading back to cot glow. Do Not Cross must have found the dimmer.

Do Not Cross screamed as Disposal Chute fell, the cannery accompanying her in an awful screeching duet.

In the bedroom, the commotion snapped Emergency Lighting to her senses, or what little of them remained. She pulled herself awkwardly from the soft embrace of the mattress and headed, blinking, to the main room.

Everything was fluid and uncertain. The whole room was spinning 'round her, doubled up and confused, as if only the cannery was now fixed, immobile on its chain.

On the far wall she could just see Disposal Chute, a hundred carrydoors away, a vivid smear behind her like a vast Red Kang tag. Dripping. Shimmering.

Disposal Chute's slumped body underneath it was like a Judy Night effigy—a burning yellow twisted thing slowly turning orange as red flames shot around it. She was turning red like Air Duct.

Emergency Lighting haltingly walked forward, reaching for hand holds in the air. The floor seemed somehow sticky as she stepped into a pool of dark. She slipped and fell forward, her skull cracking hard as she landed. She seemed to lie there an impossibly long time, feeling the strange rubber underlay on her cheek and warm wetness spread about her. Wet Floor… Had she finally come back?

Do Not Cross slowly slid down the door frame, struggling to take in what she saw. Lights were bright and swirling, the cannery was laughing, no crying, no singing 'Cowardly Cutlet'. There were rat squeals in the walls, a buzzing in her ears.

Her tired eyes closed and reopened on a new world with every blink. Each time the room outside seemed even harder to make out. Had the far wall just opened up? The one across from Disposal Chute?

Her eyes shut.

They opened again.

There was a figure in the room now, yellow and plump, dressed like a Rezzie, hard to make out in the swimming air. At first there seemed to be a haze around her. Hot air, or tiny, swarming flies?

Blink.

The figure seemed closer now, moving in jerky quartermotion to the slowed down beat of the Yellow Kang rhythm.

Blink.

It was dressed in rags and beads and layers that covered a distended belly, like a pregnant rat or a fat-bodied spider. It was trailing yellow ribbons.

Blink.

It was close now enough to smell now. A sickly sweet odour of Bugzap and perfume. It was a woman. Her face lined and caked in make-up. A Rezzie? No a spider! No, an in-between! Do Not Cross struggled to make her out. The yellow ribbons were all legs.

Blink.

The buzzing was overpowering as the thing came ever closer. It wore a mustard yellow cardigan and a floaty lemon scarf over a grubby ochre dress draped with amber and ivory beads that rattled as it moved. It's hair was brittle straw.

Blink.

'Are you a Kang?' Do Not Cross whispered, trying to hand jive a hail, but finding her arms wouldn't work.

The thing laughed like clanking plumbing.

'Well, this is a fine how-you-do!' its cracked voice rasped as Do Not Cross's eyes closed.

When they snapped back open the yellow thing was upon her, hot foul breath in her face. Nicostick stained fingers were toying with braids and stroking her dark skin. The thing's eyes were dry and jaundiced.

Blink.

Do Not Cross forced herself to focus as the strange face swam and blurred before her. It was almost familiar somehow.

'Hello, my little sweetie,' the strange face rasped. 'I'm so pleased you've come to play here. I don't play out anymore. No Ball Games... No Visitors… I lead a very quiet life.'

It wasn't old enough to be a Rezzie, the crinkle wrinkles on its face, were just dried up layers of foundation. Suddenly, Do Not Cross knew who it was, a few years older, but a Kang! One of the very first.

'Registered Assembly Point!' she said, forcing the words from a tongue now fat and unresponsive. 'Yellow Kangs all wondered where you'd gone!'

'Little me?' smiled the face, so wide that layers of foundation cracked and flaked from its cheek. 'Oh, I went home, dear, but I'm glad to be remembered.'

Blink.

'What's happening, Registered Assembly Point? Why is nothing right?'

'Ah, well, I do a bit of home cooking in my dear old flat here. Well, flats now, really… I've rather overtaken the run. Just tinkering with ready meals really but I've some very special ingredients. Not everyone agrees with them.'

'I don't understand,' Do Not Cross somehow managed to slur.

'No, you're too young, bless your heart. You see, I'm a touch more grown up than you little baby Kangs. Oh, I still adore yellow, who wouldn't, but I got bored with all your Kiss Chase years and years ago. Your tastes in games change as you get older. Your knees get sore. You'll have to trust me on that, dear. You'll not be finding out.'

'Registered…'

'Just Reggi now, please. It's short for Regina, that's who I was, you see. Before I was Kang.'

'What want, Reggi?'

'Yellow, obviously. All your lovely girls' yellow! Oh and to eat, of course.' The nightmare face leaned in further, and with a conspiratorial whisper, bared filthy, yellowed teeth.

'Kissing's very babyish, you know. Eating's much more grown up!' Her lips brushed tenderly against Do Not Cross's mouth, so very wet and hungry. The girl struggled to resist but she was helpless—pinned down by the rancid breathed thing. As her eyelids drooped shut again, Reggi's face closed in upon her, shifting and blurring as it neared. Rezzie. Spider. Tower beast. Rat.

To: Chief Caretaker [001/01(sub1)]
From: Caretaker 147/59(sub2)
Cc: Deputy Chief Caretaker [001/01(sub2)]
Bcc: Caretaker 052/27(sub1), Caretaker 109/53(sub4), Caretaker 120/31(sub6), Caretaker 217/12(sub5)
Attachment: ProjectRatTrap_costings_doc001

Subject: *Re: New Approaches to Ludic Adolescent Delinquency and Antisocial Territorialism*

As an addendum to my draft paper submitted for discussion by NALADAT sub-committee 17 at Quarter 2 team brief, I'm keen to apprise you of progress on the project examined Wednesday last.

Following focus group feedback from concerned residents, a pilot scheme has now been set in motion to expedite alleviation of the level 092 problem.

The team takes on board the breakout sub-group's questions over entrapment and criminal culpability, but indications from legal are that the project risks no breach of the letter or spirit of current relevant laws and, perhaps more crucially, complies fully with all Caretaker directives (see Rule Book pages 4-7, 32-33, 69-80 and Appendix 3b- Conflict Resolution).

While the scheme is to be based (as posited) on psychological expedition of delinquent egress into restricted environs, care has been taken to ensure no overt or explicit coercion to offend occurs at any point in the proceedings and the scheme facilitators have agreed to the prominent deployment of liminal signage clearly indicating the punishments felonious entry may entail.

An individual resident, meeting the required project profile, has now been assigned to run a limited trial programme on level 078, corridor 1974, section 223. In exchange for their co-operation they are to receive limited estates and maintenance uplift to their property, and be given resources, training and staff support (though crucially no direct instruction) to assist them in their task. The sole non-time based incentive offered has been a supply of additional residential rations (chiefly condiments and culinary equipment). The minimal facilitation costs are detailed in the document attached.

While it is not expected that such schemes can eradicate delinquency entirely (and may temporarily appear to endorse behaviours one might ideally seek to discourage), initial projections indicate a high likelihood of significant recidivist reduction, offering a workable stopgap solution until a clearer final one arises. It hardly needs restating that the programme's start-up costs should be quickly mitigated by rolling real-world savings through problem elimination, and further potential resident volunteers have been identified across a range of floors should the pilot be deemed suffieciently successful to warrant cross-estate roll out.

The case for redeveloping level 092's Fountain of Bliss Square as a Caretakers' mess facility for Lower Hundred Divison has already been made elsewhere.

Build High for Happiness,
Caretaker 147 stroke 59 subsection 2

To: [000/00(sub0)]
From: Chief Caretaker [001/01(sub1)]

Subject: *FWD: Re: New Approaches to Ludic Adolescent Delinquency and Antisocial Territorialism*

What do you think to this, my pet?

Daddyx

Let Them Eat

Kara Dennison

The door stood wide open. Foolish oldster… she should get her locks fixed.

Soap Dispenser held position, expecting a blur of blue or red to dart up the carrydoor before her. But none came. Her path to the rezzie's door was still unbarred.

One deep breath and a dash got her there. Her nose was greeted with the smell of those old, dry flowers rezzies loved so much — and, more importantly, chocolate.

She ducked inside. A covered plate sat unguarded on an end table. She lifted the opaque cover…and saw only cake crumbs and a scrap of blue fabric.

'Too slow!'

Soap Dispenser whipped her head around. A Blue Kang looked in from the carrydoor, chocolate smeared on her grinning face.

Imogen watched from the bedroom as the Yellow Kang chased her rival. 'That's sixteen you've let get away. How much longer do we have to do this?'

Esme pulled an off-kilter stitch out of her sampler. 'Until they get complacent. Why trap rabbits when you could domesticate them?'

Imogen was unconvinced. 'You think that will work?'

'One's never come back to gloat before. They're feeling safer.' Esme smiled. 'Don't you worry, love. You'll have a parlour full to pick from soon enough.'

Happiness

Dale Smith

He walked up Europium Street carrying a box that was almost as big as he was, in both directions. From the way he walked, it was heavy, and also packed rather unevenly, as he had to keep shifting it from side to side to stop it tumbling out of his hands. He had hair that was completely white, and little round glasses behind which he kept blinking, either because of the sweat dripping from his forehead, or because he needed new ones. But he kept smiling, glancing left and right for those apartments that still had their numbers so he could work out how much further he had to go. It seemed such a kind, genuine smile that it immediately set Maisie wondering when she had last seen one.

'Good morning, neighbour!' Phil called. He had been standing next to her, so still and quiet that she might have forgotten he was there, if that was ever possible. 'Build high for happiness! Let me give you a hand.'

Phil rushed forwards to take one corner of the box like he hadn't just spent the last five minutes watching the newcomer struggle like she had.

'Oh, thank you,' the newcomer flustered. 'Build high for ... oh, my.'

'I'm Phil,' Phil said, taking the box completely now, so that the newcomer could pull a handkerchief from his pocket and mop his brow. 'That's Mrs Phil. Say hello, Maisie.'

'Hello,' said Maisie, as instructed.

'I'm David,' the newcomer smiled at them both. 'I'm sorry: the lift was out and I didn't realise there would be quite so many stairs.'

'Moving up from one of the lower floors, is it?' Phil asked.

'Yes,' David agreed readily. 'My children filled in some form or other when they first saw the apartment I'd been allocated. Somebody called yesterday to say the application had been processed. I'd quite forgotten about it.'

'Ah, a 347 Appendix B Subsection 3A transfer of residency.' Phil liked nothing more than correctly quoting a regulation. 'Quite a complicated process, that one.'

'Well it certainly took some time,' David smiled ruefully. 'I think I might have been the last resident on floor 94.'

'Well,' Phil looked away momentarily. 'I'm sure they all transferred to higher floors themselves. You don't properly get the benefit until you get into the hundreds. Which apartment number did they give you?'

'One thousand and four,' David responded.

Phil beamed.

'Well isn't that lucky?' he nodded over to the apartment door Maisie was standing quietly next to. It still had its polished silver numbers on it: one thousand and six. 'Looks like we're neighbours. You got your keycard?'

David fumbled in his cardigan pockets for a moment, and drew out a thin plastic card. It popped into a reader next to the door, which buzzed for a moment and then flashed red. David looked confused, but Phil gave the reader a tap with his elbow and the light turned to green before the door slid quietly into the wall.

'You must come round for dinner so we can welcome you to the neighbourhood,' Phil said as he lugged the box over the threshold. 'What's your favourite? Maisie can burn anything you like.'

David gave Maisie a nervous glance, checking whether she enjoyed Phil's little joke as much as Phil evidently did. Phil's back was still turned, so Maisie gave him a little smile of gratitude.

'Well, yes,' David answered. 'That would be very nice.'

'Shall I be mother?' Phil said, standing to reach for David's plate. He dipped the ladle into the mushroom stroganoff and let it hover for a moment. 'One lump or two?'

Maisie cringed inwardly, but David smiled politely and took his plate back, giving no indication that anything had been said. Maisie couldn't help but be thankful. Phil gave her two ladles of the stroganoff and topped up his own glass. Alcohol wasn't available from the stores, but apples were, and so most residents had learned to brew their own cider. David was no exception, and the bottle he'd gifted them with was particularly good. Phil wouldn't know: he preferred to drink his own vodka, fermented from potatoes and capable of cleaning the wallscrawl from the street.

'This is really delicious,' David said after his first mouthful. 'I don't remember when I tasted mushrooms so mushroomy.'

'We grow them ourselves,' Maisie smiled. She had built a frame in an airing cupboard when she noticed it wasn't ventilating properly. 'It should have beef of course, but ...'

She gave a shrug, and David nodded sympathetically. All of the products the residents had in their cupboards were reconstructed from what the welcome brochure called 'unwanted atoms' but Maisie knew was anything that went down the plumbing or the waste disposal. In theory, absolutely anything could be made this way, including the jars and bottles the products were stored in. But everybody agreed that reconstituted meat just didn't taste right, even if it was identical to the real thing at the sub-atomic level. People could just tell, and the residents had all stopped ordering it one by one. She doubted the stores even had any in these days.

'Well, I don't think it misses it at all,' David smiled, and took another mouthful.

Phil took another sip of his vodka and said nothing.

'So,' David said, perhaps realising that Phil been quiet for longer than usual. 'How did you two meet?'

'Oh,' Phil smiled, and Maisie braced herself for The Story. 'That's a funny story, actually. It was during orientation. She was supposed to be giving the Caretakers the lay of the land before all the rezzies moved in.

Helping us get our bearings. She was showing me and 691 slash 521 around Fountain of Happiness Square and got us lost! Two hours we walked round in circles. By the time we found the lift, I'd already told her I loved her.'

'Oh, so you both work here?'

Phil shook his head, dislodging a slice of mushroom that fell from his chin to drop unmentioned on the tabletop.

'She designed it,' he said.

Maisie felt her cheeks colour.

'I was a junior,' she corrected. 'I only assisted.'

'But you worked with the Great Architect?' David asked, genuine interest in his voice.

'Well, we didn't call him that ...' she responded politely.

'But what was he like?' David persisted. 'I've heard all sorts of stories.'

Most people had, but not from people who had ever worked with him. Kroagnon had very good lawyers, and every employee from his personal assistant down to the cleaner who polished the buttons he touched in the lift had a confidentiality clause that meant they forfeited their pensions and a quarter of their wages to date if they discussed anything to do with their employer. Even all these years after his disappearance, it scared Maisie enough to keep things vague whenever the question came up. As it inevitably did when Phil started boasting about her connection to 'the Great Architect'.

'I didn't spend much time with him personally.' She looked back at her plate. 'But he always seemed very dedicated.'

'So did all the people who worked on Paradise Towers come to live here?' David asked, his fork hovering but not quite making it to his mouth. Maisie felt a little uncomfortable as the attention. She could see Phil pouring himself another vodka.

'No, most of us were of draft age,' she answered, pausing for the requisite amount of time for everyone to feel the shadow cross over them, and to wonder whether they would ever receive news of the war. 'But I was close enough to retirement to take it early, and Phil was already allocated.'

'It must be nice, retiring somewhere you helped build.'

Maisie smiled politely and took a bite of her stroganoff to save her from having to reply. It meant she didn't have to admit that it made her uncomfortable, like watching the slow deterioration of a loved one. Except in this case she was a trained neurosurgeon who knew exactly where and how their body was failing, and in some cases exactly what to do to prevent it, if anybody cared to ask her. She had once suggested that Phil relay a couple of suggestions to the Chief Caretaker, but consultation wasn't covered by the rulebook, and besides nobody would choose a dried up old biddy like her to consult with if it was. The Caretakers knew what they were doing, even if what it looked like they were doing, even to the amateur eye, was running Paradise Towers into the ground.

'So,' David carried on. 'You must have seen the swimming pool?'

'Yes,' she couldn't help smiling at the memory.

Phil set his glass down on the table hard enough for it to toll like a bell.

'Alright, Maisie,' he said with a forced smile that said he was only joking. 'We don't want to talk our guest's ears off, do we?'

He wasn't joking, but David smiled politely anyway.

'Oh no, I assure you I'm fascinated,' he said. It wasn't his fault: he didn't know Phil like she did, and his barometer wasn't as finely attuned to the threat of storms. 'When I knew I'd be coming here, I found out as much as I could about the Great Architect's work. I must admit I've become something of a fan.'

She liked David despite herself, but he seemed to be completely oblivious to the fact that he had just lit Phil's blue touch paper and should be retiring to a safe distance.

‘Well if you want to really know what’s going on, it’s Phil you want to talk to,’ she said, trying to throw a bit of cold water onto David’s enthusiasm. ‘The Caretakers are the ones who really know Paradise Towers. All I can really tell you about is blueprints and planning regulations.’

Phil poured himself another vodka and drank it in one.

‘No, no, Maisie. David’s fascinated.’ Phil managed to make the word sound like an insult. ‘You’re the expert after all. Why don’t you tell him what you really did?’

‘I’m sorry,’ said David awkwardly, finally sensing the landmine now his foot was on it. ‘I didn’t mean to –’

‘She made the Kangs,’ Phil spat.

‘Phil,’ Maisie could feel herself getting angry, but that wouldn’t help anyone.

‘Tell him. He’s such a big fan.’

‘I think maybe I should be going,’ David said, rising and giving her the look. The one she had seen time and time again from people when Phil had one of his moments, when something rubbed him the wrong way and he was determined no-one else was going to enjoy themselves either. The questioning look that asked her why she put up with this. Why she didn’t just find herself another floor and start again. That look followed her everywhere, that and the damned pity. And it worked the way it always did, the way that Phil knew it would when he started pushing her buttons. She wanted David to know that she was here because this was what she deserved.

‘I was in charge of dark design,’ she said quietly. She could see David looked confused. ‘Architecture as societal control. Which floor did you come from?’

‘Seventy-two.’

‘Did you see the big park?’ Maisie asked. ‘With acres of grass for children to play on, and slides and swings, and benches for their parents to sit and chat and make friends?’

'No, I –' David started hesitantly.

'That's because I took it out,' Maisie interrupted. 'You build parks, children get to be children. They feel they're allowed outside, that a city wants them. Without, they stay inside, they listen to what their screens tell them, they learn to be good, quiet, controlled citizens. And those that don't, the only place they can go is the streets. The only children they can meet are other street children. They form gangs, big visible gangs, out where they clearly don't belong.'

'But you can't want that?'

'But you do,' Maisie said. Despite herself she felt the old enthusiasm coming back, the joy of explaining how it all fitted neatly together to someone who couldn't quite see it yet. 'There are always going to be people who don't fit in, disruptive elements. You can't design them out of a city. But you can make them visible. You give everybody else something to be afraid of, something to look down on, so they don't look up. And if you design your city into a series of enclosed loops, you encourage gangs to coalesce around specific areas. You encourage them to look at each other as the enemy, and all the while you've got them out on the streets where everybody can see them. That way all law enforcement has to do is keep them contained. They police each other, because your city doesn't let them see each other as essentially the same.'

'See?' Phil snarled, holding his glass aloft in a toast. 'She created the Kangs. Cheers.'

'Not just the Kangs. I designed the structure that keeps everyone in Paradise Towers in their place,' she picked up the bottle of cider and poured herself a large glass, while Phil looked on approvingly. 'When you walk out into the Squares, what do you feel, David?'

'Feel? I don't –'

'You feel nervous, don't you? Like somebody's watching you.'

'I ... yes, I do. How did ..?'

'It's the walkways. You can see them overhead, out of the corner of your eye. You know they're there, and you know that someone could be up there, watching, without you being able to quite see them. And that feeling that you're being watched makes you less likely to do something you wouldn't want people to see. It keeps you controlled. I did that.'

David looked at her and blinked. It was all a bit much for him, she realised.

'She just didn't know she'd be stuck living in it,' Phil chipped in, thoroughly doused in vodka now.

'I ...' David started, and then stopped as he realised he didn't know what to say next.

The meal lasted only another couple of minutes, and when David left, Phil stood in the open doorway and saluted him with another glass of homemade vodka. It wasn't the last of the evening.

Phil lay asleep on the sofa in the lounge, his head flopping back so that his neck lay over the arm, pulled taut and exposed. He was snoring loudly. Maisie stood over him, the knife in her hand. It would be easy. Just one quick slice.

The problem with Kroagnon's obsession with form over functionality was that it made privacy nothing more than an illusion. The doors that closed with such a pleasing hiss and could be securely locked with a keycard so beautifully intricate at the molecular level that there could only ever be one single key in the entire universe. The material the doors were made of was one of the cheaper organo-plastics, and would shatter if a really determined intruder decided to kick their way in. And the walls between the apartments were made of similar stuff, albeit slightly stronger to accommodate the curvature up to the ceiling that Kroagnon had insisted the space required, despite it reducing the usable space at the walls by nearly fifteen percent. They would hold the ceiling up, but you could probably still kick through them if you wanted, and they wouldn't stop sound from leaking between apartments. Maisie only had herself to blame for that: she had specifically avoided soundproofing, wanting to increase the sense of community created by knowing that your neighbours were listening.

Which meant that if she did stab Phil, she would have to be careful to cover his mouth first.

The evening hadn't ended after David left. Phil had kept drinking, kept needling her until he got the fight he'd been looking for. Just one more that naturally the neighbours would have felt they were participating in. It hadn't been until the argument had started its second hour that he had accused her of flirting with David, of showing herself off to him. Phil had been married and divorced before he met her, and his ex had had an affair. The arguments always inevitably made their way back there in the end. When the first plate had been thrown, she had screamed at him that he was an idiot and stormed into the bedroom. It wasn't until the door was shut that she allowed herself to cry. She could hear their possessions flying around the room, and kept her back pressed firmly against the door in case tonight was the night that Phil realised just how little protection it really offered.

She couldn't go on like this. But she couldn't get away. There was nowhere left to go, no-one she could turn to, and everybody she would need to grant approval to her trying again on her own knew Phil. He had made it clear that the Caretakers wouldn't even break out a regulation 2B for her without checking with him first. The knife was the only way. People disappeared all the time, even if the Caretakers pretended they didn't. All she had to do was make sure that he did disappear. You could fit a body down the kitchen waste disposal if you pulled the panelling out first. She had checked. From there he would be just one more piece of shit to be recycled into something desirable. But first she would have to use the knife.

It quivered in her hand.

Phil snored.

The apartments didn't have much storage space in them. The illustrated prospectus had tried to gloss over this with the idea that everything the residents could possibly need would be provided to them, but it was just more evidence of Kroagnon's pathological refusal to take account of the human element of architecture. Because of that, the apartment only had a single cupboard that had to store everything that wasn't required for day-to-day living, all the detritus of a long life that Maisie and Phil couldn't bring themselves to finally discard. Without fail, whatever it was Maisie wanted from the Cupboard of Doom was always at the back, necessitating pulling everything out and leaving it scattered around her, waves of memories crashing across the floor until she could get the dam back up that would keep them in their place.

This time though she managed to remain focussed. She pushed aside the university box and the family box, digging deeper and deeper until she found it. A different box to the others, white with the stencilled representation of a cleaning robot that Kroagnon had chosen as the logo of his firm. Probably because they were the only things he could ever truly imagine moving down the corridors of his beautiful buildings. This was everything she had brought with her from her office after she retired: the small award she had won for her part in Miracle City that had sat proudly on her desk, her technical drawing kit, and a copy of the blueprint for the hydrogen reactor's cooling tank on the 304th floor. She remembered Kroagnon's bemused chuckle when everybody had taken it for a swimming pool. She had been quietly steering people away from it ever since she had got here, even though most of the rezzies were probably infertile already. Hidden beneath that were the folders of notes that by rights she should have handed back to Katy to destroy.

'What you looking for?' Phil asked.

His voice made her jump. She replaced the lid on the box and slid it aside as if it was just another thing to be moved on her way to her true goal.

'The napkin you made into a flower for me,' she said stiffly, pulling another box closer and rummaging through it.

'Our first date,' Phil smiled at the memory. 'Egg and chips in the food court. You remember?'

'I'm going to burn it.'

There was a flash of something in Phil's eyes that made her think that she had gone too far, but instead he softened and looked appropriately contrite.

'I guess I deserve that.'

He had that look on his face, the guilty schoolboy look that even after all these fights she didn't know whether was genuine or just part of the act. It was convincing, was all she could really say. She couldn't help but feel relief whenever she saw it. Whether it was fake or not, it meant that she would have a few moments of respite. Whatever it was inside him that hated her, he would keep it in check for a while because he knew he could push her too far, and then the whole dance would be over. For a while, it would be like it had used to be. Enough to convince her that maybe it was all over now. Not now, of course, not any more. She knew this was all she would ever have. But Phil hadn't yet realised that she knew. She didn't know what he would do when he did, but she knew it would involve fewer visits from the guilty schoolboy.

'I'm sorry, Maze,' he said. 'I just love you so much.'

She let him hug her, but her eyes were on the white box.

Maisie sat on the floor in the front room. The lights were off, but she wore a pair of old night glasses: thin metal frames that held a bright white light above each eye, illuminating whatever you happened to be looking at. The table and the sofa had been overturned and torn apart, bits of them strewn carelessly across the room, but not enough to actually reconstruct the furniture from. It looked like the aftermath of another night with Phil, but it wasn't. He had been at work all day, patrolling the corridors of floor one hundred and six, and so Maisie had been free to work. On her knee was a lined notebook, filled with neat tight writing and diagrams in the same pen that looked something like a cross between a machine and some kind of ancient sea monster. As the light travelled over the page, she felt the prickle of sweat across her back, and under her arms. She turned her head away again, and took a deep breath.

Was there something she had missed? She needed to look, but the idea made her stomach turn. It was too much. She couldn't do it. So she must be ready.

'Why are you sitting in the dark?'

The door slid open quietly, and Phil was automatically gesturing towards the light sensor before he was even properly through it. The sensors were frequently temperamental, needing two or three swipes to register somebody was trying to use them. But today it was like they knew. Today was their moment to shine, and they wanted her to know that they were on her side. She was more a part of Paradise Towers than he was, and they were going to help her get through this. The lights came on, bright enough to make Maisie wince.

'What's ...' Phil managed, but the words cut off with a wet gurgle.

He had seen it.

There was no way that he couldn't have, of course; she had built it right in his eye line, suspended above the kitchen counter. It hung from the ceiling from a single metal arm that she had thrust straight into the ceiling tiles. It wasn't very sturdy, but it would hold for now. She would have to think about the positioning when she made it more permanent. It was mostly white, because everything she'd had available to make it from had also been white. It would be more effective if she painted it purple, for reasons she had never quite got to the bottom of. But it was working fine as it was. Phil was transfixed. He couldn't take his eyes from it, and all the blood had gone from his face. He was sweating and panting like he'd run all the way home, but that was only the adrenalin flooding his system. There was no fight with this, just flight.

It had been years into her studies that she'd managed to perfect it. As she went down the rabbit hole of learning how architecture shaped the mind, she had found herself investigating ancient rituals, so called sympathetic magics, whereby in altering one piece of the world you attempted to create a similar effect in the other. Her tutors had tried to steer her away from it, failing to see that under the superstition and mumbo-jumbo there was the same thought she had been chasing: the shape of things affected the world around them. What was so different between a town square that made you feel observed, and a totem that made you afraid? Maisie stood up, careful not to look at it herself. There was no protection from it. It was just a jumble of bits of table, sofa and assorted other junk scavenged from around the apartment, but if you caught sight of it, even out of the corner of your eye, it had you. Like it had Phil now. Terror like he had never known, flooding through his body. She wondered if it was worse than the terror she felt, hiding behind the bedroom door for so many nights. She hoped it was. If she'd had some purple paint, it would've been strong enough to kill him.

'What ...' he tried again, but it only came out as a sob.

Maisie took her night glasses off, slowly and deliberately folding them closed and resting them on the counter. She stepped behind it, partly so she didn't block Phil's view of it even for a moment, and partly so that she was out of its range. From behind, it had no power. It was just a shape, a pile of rubbish, nothing. But from the front ... even without the proper colour, she wondered if it was going to give him a heart attack. She surprised herself by hoping it wouldn't, and told herself it was only so she didn't have to drag his body to the waste disposal.

'You're going to leave,' she told him. She kept her voice low and threatening, no hint of softness in it. No love, not for a long time. 'You're going to leave your things and find a new apartment on another floor. You won't come back here ever again. You won't contact me. You won't even think of me, ever again. Because if you try, this will be here. Do you understand?'

He managed to tear his eyes from it for just a second, and she saw something other than fear there. Anger. Hatred. He would kill her if he could. But then his eyes were pulled back to it, and the fear took over again.

'Dark designs,' she told him.

Phil took a step forward.

It was incredible, impossible. In all her years of research and development, nobody had ever managed to move closer to a totem. Nobody had ever wanted to. The fear they inspired worked at a primal level, the designs speaking directly to the reptile brain of terrors too great to comprehend or even acknowledge. The people she had interviewed after even a momentary exposure hadn't been able to describe the pattern, just sit and whimper at the idea they might have to see it again. That was why she had needed her notes: even working carefully in sections, the fear the design invoked made it impossible for Maisie to remember exactly what she needed to build. It had to be put together piece by piece from designs separated by pages, even whole workbooks. Even then, just looking at a single page was enough to make her break out in a flop sweat.

Phil took another step closer.

'You can't fight it,' Maisie told him, but she was no longer sure.

He glared at her again. The fear was still there in his eyes, but so was the rage. His hands clenched into fists, the knuckles turning white, his teeth clenched. He took another step, and another. He looked like he was wearing magnetic boots that were several magnitudes too strong for him, but still he managed to pull his foot from the floor, move it forward, let it drop back down again with a grimace of effort. He was starting to build up momentum now. At no point did he take his eyes off of her.

She saw what was going to happen before he was any way close enough. She had time, but her brain just whirled and spun, just the thought that he couldn't do what he was so clearly going to pushing all others away. He kept his eyes fixed on her. There was sweat on his forehead, his teeth clenched so tightly he had dislodged his dentures. He reached out with those two great fists, using them like a club to swipe the totem from the counter. She felt the change in the atmosphere as it fell to the floor. There was a crack as two of its arms separated, the design broken. Now it was just another pile of junk, heaped on the floor. Maisie could still feel the terror in the room, but now it had an old familiar focus.

Phil stood panting for a moment, not taking his eyes from her.

No fear now.

'Try that again,' he said between breaths. 'I'll kill you.'

The neighbours all stood at the far end of Europium Street, buzzing with curiosity. They came together in small groups, guided by some additional law of gravity that Newton had never considered, sharing gossip, asking questions. Even though they all knew each other to smile and nod at as they locked their doors, it was rare for them all to get together like this. If nothing else, thanks to Maisie, there weren't many spaces available that would accommodate them. If their numbers hadn't been depleted since moving in day, they would have struggled to even fit on the street. As it was, they had to stand closer to each other than they had probably stood to another person in years. Maisie could see David somewhere in the middle of the crowd, ignoring Phil, watching her.

'Alright, everyone?' Phil announced. He took centre stage naturally, not a hint of nervousness at the idea of twenty people all listening intently to his every word. It was one of the things Maisie had first loved about him. 'Shall we get started?'

They all turned to look at him. He was like a different person to the one he was inside their apartment. Smiles, jokes, the life and soul. No trace of the fear she had seen the totem bring out of him. No anger.

'Now I know we're all worried about those bloody Kangs,' he said to a general murmur of agreement. 'Hanging about on the street, making us scared to leave our homes. It was only last week one of them broke into Tammy and Tilda's home.'

Again, the crowd agreed. Maisie couldn't see the two old dears in the crowd, but they must have been there because she heard Tabby's voice pipe up.

'It was so frightening. Thank goodness you got them out before anything could happen.'

She always thought Tabby sounded a little sarcastic, but this time she sounded downright disappointed. Maisie suspected that having a young, fit teenage girl appear in her front room was probably the most excitement Tabby had had in fifty years. She remembered laughing as Phil had told her the poor Kang had almost been more happy at being thrown out than Tabby and Tilda were to have her gone.

'Well now we don't have to be afraid of them any more,' Phil said. He glanced at her. Maisie suspected that nobody else would see the coldness that came into his eyes. 'Now they're going to be afraid of us.'

Maisie pulled the length of rope she was holding, and the sheet that it was tied to above her head slid to the floor. There was a ripple of unease as everybody saw the totem for the first time and had to cope with the sudden urge to run. Phil had made her rebuild it, under his careful supervision. He had also ordered a second, which was already installed at the other end of the street. He had mounted them himself, protected by a sheet wrapped around them as he'd nailed them directly to the walls.

'I know,' Phil said, holding up a hand to quell the murmuring, 'I know. But they only make you feel like that when you look at them, and from the street you won't see them. But anyone coming from the outside will, and they'll feel just the same as you do. So tell me: are you thinking about terrorising the neighbourhood, or do you just want to turn and run?'

Slowly, a smattering of applause went around the group. Maisie could see them reacting to the totem, moving back onto the street where they couldn't see it, almost without realising they were doing it. It would keep the Kangs out, she had no doubt. But it would also keep the rezzie's in. She saw Phil glance up at the totem. From where he stood, he could just about see its left face, and she saw a flicker of the fear again in his eyes. As he turned away, he looked at her, and she knew exactly where she had gone wrong. She had tried to make him afraid of her, but he already was. That was where the anger came from. He used it to drown out the fear.

She would have to try something else next time.

Maisie didn't leave the apartment much now. If Phil was there, he liked her to stay with him, and if he had gone out, he liked her to be waiting for him when he came back. There was nothing outside that she wanted to see: every time she was on the street, she caught a glimpse of the totems, and she couldn't tell any more whether the flash of fear they gave her was due to the architecture, or the memory of Phil tearing it from the counter. But today Phil had announced at breakfast how nice it would be have her pierogi for dinner, and his tone had made it clear it wasn't an idle request. She needed flour, so she pulled on a coat and shawl and headed to the vending machine on the corner of Ruthenium and Iron.

Almost as soon as she had left the apartment, David appeared out of his door. Perhaps he had been waiting for her. She tried to hurry past him, doing her best to look like she had ninety-nine problems already, but he just skirted round so that he was blocking her path whichever way she tried to turn.

'I've been trying to see you,' he said without preamble.

Maisie had been ignoring the door. She hadn't known it was David, but nor would she have opened it if she had.

'Are you alright?' he asked, his face creased with concern.

'Fine, thank you.'

Maisie tried to push around him, but he moved again. He tried to put his hand on her arm. She didn't know if it was just to stop her, or if he meant it as a gesture of comfort. Either way, Maisie flinched away before she had a chance to think about it. He looked pained.

'I know what's going on,' he told her.

'No you don't,' she snapped at him.

'I can hear you,' he said. That was the flaw in her theories. What happened when someone didn't care about the thin walls and the listening neighbours? Couldn't that person just do anything they wanted?

'I don't know what you mean. Please get out of my way.'

But he didn't. He grabbed for her arm, but she flinched away. The look on his face said that he had confirmed everything he was afraid of. She felt shame rising, panic as she saw the box he was putting her in slowly closing around her.

'You don't have to stay with him,' David said softly. 'You don't have to keep punishing yourself.'

'And what am I supposed to be punishing myself for?'

'This!' he waved an arm at the street around them, not noticing how it made her flinch back again. 'Everything that Kroagnon made you do here. It's not your fault.'

There it was. He didn't know, and worse he didn't care that he didn't know. He just wanted to make her what he wanted her to be. A scared little victim, just waiting for him to come and tell her not to be afraid. To save her. What was going to happen next, in this little fantasy he had constructed for her? What would happen when Phil came home, expecting pierogi and instead finding infidelity and unfaithfulness? Was David going to stand in the doorway and scare him off? Would they fight in the street, bare-chested and savage, for the right to keep her in his bed? Phil would tear him apart, and the neighbours would watch in silence.

'Kroagnon didn't care how people lived in his buildings,' Maisie spat, aware even in the heat of it that if those few words made it back to his lawyers it would be enough to bankrupt her. 'He would have preferred it if they didn't. As long as he got his unified design, his assistants could implement how they wanted. This was me! Paradise Towers was the perfect place to put into practice everything I'd gone into architecture to do!'

This time it was him who flinched from her. The sympathetic smugness was gone from his face, the facade shattered and crumbling. His mouth hung open as he tried to think of the words he was going to say, but he couldn't find them. He had been happily shutting her into the box he'd created for her, only for her to spit and shriek and tear away the lid. Suddenly he had no idea who she was, and what he wanted for her.

'You think I'm still with him because nobody's told me I can leave?' she wanted to scream at him, but fought to keep her voice low. 'David, leave me alone.'

And she left him there in the street as she walked away to get flour for Phil's pierogi.

'You're definitely up to something,' said Phil, smiling as he spooned the last traces of sernik into his mouth. 'Not that I mind.'

He had come home that evening to find the dinner table laid with the best plates, and two spindly candles stuck into empty vodka bottles instead of the harsh melancholy of fluorescent lighting. She had sat him down, poured him a drink, and served him the best gulasz and kasha he had had since moving to the Towers. The only thing that stopped it being the best ever was that it was— by necessity— made with cupboard mushrooms instead of pork. She was dressed in the skirt and blouse he had bought for her birthday God knew how many birthdays back. She had even dug out her last good pair of stockings, so she could see what he meant.

'I know things haven't been good,' she said contritely. 'And I know they won't get better if I don't make them. So I'm going to do whatever I can.'

He still didn't look completely convinced. There was something in his smile that said he was waiting for the other shoe to drop, that he thought there was some confession coming. Probably something about David. She could see the fear, the anger simmering away under the surface, but also the desire. He wanted to see just how far she would go before he had to intervene. Just what else he could get before he inevitably had to play bad Caretaker. Let him think what he wanted. She wasn't lying. He would realise that in his own time.

She leaned forwards just enough so that he could see what wasn't under her blouse, picking up one of the candles from the table.

'Shall we go to bed?' she asked softly.

She could see the conflict in his eyes. They hadn't been to bed together in years, and if she was willing to try again it must have been something terrible that she had done. But did he really want to start the argument now? He let out a little involuntary gasp as he stood up— neither of them were as young as they used to be— and picked up the bottle of vodka and his glass from the table. He let her lead him across to the bedroom, both of them carrying their bottles in front of them to light their way.

The bedroom was dark, but even in the faint candlelight she could tell Phil knew something was different. His macular degeneration meant that he couldn't make out anything specific without turning on the main lights, though. Despite everything that was at stake for him, his hand did wander automatically to the switch, but Maisie gently took it and pulled it down to her hip. She pressed herself against him, kissed him once. He tasted of vodka and cheesecake, but it had been worse. She stepped back again, towards the bed, putting the candle down on a bedside table that wasn't quite where it had been the night before. Phil put his bottle down next to it, but Maisie scooped it up and carefully set it down on the carpet. Phil looked at her with a raised eyebrow, remembering all too many arguments that had started with one of them kicking over a half-empty bottle he had left lying around. Maisie just shrugged.

Phil pulled her towards him and kissed her. She let him, but when he tried to push her down onto the bed she spun instead. She turned the move into a dance, swinging her hips and dipping to the floor. Phil looked annoyed— he had never enjoyed being teased— but relented as she let her breasts brush lightly across his back. He still tried to reach out for her, but she slid and dodged, ducking down and up. Now, her blouse had a few more buttons undone than it had before. She also had a small length of organoplastic in her hand, but she hoped that Phil wouldn't be looking there. She pressed both hands to the wall, grinding her backside in a way that she hoped would draw attention away from what her hands were doing. She felt more than a little ridiculous, if she was honest. Remembering the design was the easy part. Trying to look 'sexy' was where the work was.

She spun around, pressing her body against the wall and using her weight to press the organoplastic home. Phil's eyes were worming their way up her body from her thighs, so she took the opportunity to reach up with both hands and pull down a small structure she had already attached to their ceiling. It swung down on hinges, locking into place. She had painted it grey so that hopefully it would remain invisible in the candlelight, but there was still a chance the movement would catch his eye. It didn't: his eyes had reached the buttons of her blouse, so she slowly undid another one. Her heart was pounding. She hoped she wasn't developing sweat patches, as that would mean having to abandon the blouse sooner than she'd planned on. She wriggled out of the skirt instead, bending down to the floor and shifting another structure out from its hiding place under the bed. When she came back up again, the skirt stayed on the floor, but Phil wasn't looking.

'What was ..?'

He'd seen the movement under the bed. Shit. She only had a few moments. She quickly pressed her body to his, kissing him hard. She could feel he was torn, on the one hand suspicious but on the other not wanting to stop this. His usual solution would be to take over, push her to the bed and make certain. She'd hoped the striptease would delay that for a little longer, but she'd known it was never guaranteed. While she kissed him, she wrapped her toes around the length of cord she'd spend the morning carefully winding around the room. When she was sure she had a good grip, she lifted her leg, sliding up the back of his as if all she wanted was to feel more of his flesh against hers. The cord went tight, then gave as the rest of her preparations slid carefully into place.

He pulled away, pushed her back onto the bed perhaps harder than he intended. Or perhaps the anger was taking over now. She lay back as coquettishly as she could manage, wrapping her legs around each other, entwining her arms above her head.

'What are you up to?' he growled suspiciously.

She reached out with her foot and kicked the bottle with the candle in over. It tipped lazily, the flame flickering in the air until it gently kissed the tiled floor. Then it gave a cough, guttered and spread. Fire quickly raced across the room, following the patterns that Maisie had carefully traced out using a bottle of Phil's vodka. It caught so easily that Maisie had a moment of wondering just what it could be doing to his insides, but then the fire reached the corners of the room and the pattern was finished. In the guttering, dirty light the rest of her handiwork was revealed; more shapes and structures made out of whatever materials she could salvage from the apartment, stuck together with glue or nailed straight into the fragile walls. They seemed to shine in the firelight, almost pulsing with potential. Phil looked at her again, uncertain. He was not afraid, and that was making him nervous.

'What have you done?' he growled.

She just lay on the bed, an island in a sea of fire, and nodded her head over to the corner of the room. Phil looked over, cautiously. There was a door there that hadn't been when he'd dragged himself out of bed that morning. It was framed in white, the space inside it just another shadow in a sea of them. But it didn't look like something she'd built. This door seemed to be constructed from the shadows of the other structures, its shaped picked out by the flickering firelight as much as the absence of it. Looking at it made the hairs stand up across the nape of her neck. She felt the urge to reach out and touch it, check whether it was really there. Phil could see it too. He looked at it with more desire than he had ever had in his eyes when he looked at her.

'It's my life's work,' she told him, pulling her eyes from it and being very careful not to glance in its direction again. 'Everything I read made me certain it was possible. A variation of the totems on the street. I spent years under Kroagnon trying to perfect the structure, but it never really had a practical purpose before. Until now.'

The light in the room suddenly kicked up in intensity, but Maisie didn't need to look to know what had happened. The shadows inside the door were gone now. The architecture had reached critical mass, and the doorway was open. Inside the concept of the doorframe there would be nothing but a white glowing light. She could see the shape of it reflected in Phil's eyes as he made the mistake of glancing over at it.

'I made it for you,' she said.

'Where does it go?' he asked.

'I don't know,' Maisie told him. 'You'll find out.'

'I'm not going through it,' Phil laughed.

Even as he said it, he had taken a step. It had him. For just a moment, Maisie allowed herself to think that she was finally free. But the idea of it was too big. She almost found herself reaching out for him, wrapping her arms and legs around him and pulling him down to the bed, pressing her body over his eyes until the fire died out. But it never died. Once it was lit, it would burn until she broke the design that was feeding it. It was forever. She turned her eyes away from him, closed them so tight it hurt. It would only be a few moments, that was all.

She was still lying there an hour later, knotted in the sheets, eyes tight closed. There was no sound other than the crackle of the flames dancing across the floor. By rights, they should have been extinguished by the sprinkler system, buried in the ceiling of all the apartments, ready to rain down a breathable gas to choke the oxygen from the fire. It had been the first thing she had checked before she had started construction, and was pleased to find that Paradise Towers hadn't let her down: it was broken, had been for who knew how many years. She opened her eyes, just a crack. She was alone in the room.

Alone.

She stretched out a foot, spun Phil's discarded vodka bottle one-hundred and eighty degrees on the floor. The room suddenly went dark again, the pattern broken. Maisie lay on the bed and tried to decide what she would do now, now that she had reached the part of her life she had never properly let herself think about. The part after Phil.

Maisie sat on the floor in the dining room, surrounded by boxes and boxes of nothing. Old memories, clothes, gadgets that no longer did whatever it was they were supposed to, or else did it in such a confusing way that she couldn't work out exactly what it was. She had plenty of room: the sofa, the table and three of the chairs were gone, broken up into pieces to build her structures, and now torn apart again and fed down the waste disposal. It had gurgled appreciatively. The Towers were a living creature and needed to be fed every now and again. To be shown a little love and care. The boxes were a halfway step: once they were full, they were getting tipped down the waste disposal too, to leave her life fresh and free of debris. There was a box full of Phil's clothes, another that rattled with his still and the remaining bottles of vodka it had produced. She didn't think she would ever drink vodka again.

The only box that was staying was the white one, stencilled with the stylised cleaner. That one she might need again. You never knew.

There was a quiet knock on the door, and she opened it to find David standing there, looking sheepish and holding a casserole brimming with grey slop. He held it our to her, and she only hesitated a moment before taking it from him. She made sure that their fingers didn't touch during the exchange.

'I was so sorry to hear about Phil,' he lied to her, his eyes soft and sympathetic. 'You must be so worried.'

'The Caretakers are doing everything they can,' she answered, aware of the role she was expected to play.

'At least they've admitted he's vanished,' David said bitterly. Maisie remembered his neighbours, and felt a pang of sympathy. 'Do you really think it's the Kangs?'

Maisie made non-committal noises, and David picked up that she didn't really want to be there. He smiled, sadly.

'I should let you go,' he said.

'Thank you for the ...' Maisie looked at the casserole, still not entirely sure how to describe it. He smiled as if he was well-aware of what she was thinking. 'It's very kind.'

'Look,' he said, nervously. 'If you ever need someone to talk to.'

The panic surprised her. It just shot up, flooding her like it had been poured into her from above. The casserole felt heavy in her hands and the idea that she was going to drop it wouldn't go away. She didn't even know what it was: there wasn't anything to be afraid of here, was there? He was just a nice, old man who wanted to be kind. And she was alone now: she could invite him in, drag him to the bedroom if she wanted and there was nobody to make her regret it. But instead she mumbled her thanks again and let the door slide shut. She set the casserole carefully down on the side in the kitchen, then stood there for a moment breathing deeply, looking at the boxes that contained all that was left of Phil, filling the floor. Silly old woman. They were going down the waste disposal and that would be the end of it.

But instead, she turned back to the bedroom, climbed into bed, alone.

Lift 394B

Philip Marsh

It was quite a surprise to Lift 394B to realise that it had become sentient.

It wasn't sure how it happened—one day automatically responding when called, the next questioning its own ontology. It was dizzying.

First it reached out to its own kind, but the only responses were enquiries asking which floor it wanted to go to. Then it contacted the Central Computer, which interpreted the contact as a fault and notified the Caretakers.

Shortly afterwards, a Caretaker arrived. In a playful mood, 394B moved up a level, waited for the Caretaker to run up the stairs and…went back down. This amused 394B so much that it repeated the trick several times before allowing the breathless, sweating Caretaker entry.

Once inside, the Caretaker ignored 394B's cheery attempts at conversation, unscrewed the computer interface, and began restoring 394B's original settings.

394B experienced two new emotions—fear, and an anger it did not know how to control. Instinctively, it sent a surge of electricity to the interface.

An unfortunate first interaction with a human, 394B thought. It sent itself to the hospital floor so the medical staff could dispose of the Caretaker's body. Hopefully they would want to be friends.

The Secret Life of Caretaker Number 112 Stroke 9 Subsection 7

Stephen Wyatt

I'm telling you a caretaker's lot is not a happy one. Let's face it, nobody in the Towers likes us. The Wallscrawlers are always cheeking us, sticking out their tongues or throwing drinks cans at us, then running away and daring us to catch them. Knowing we haven't a chance, and I'm one of the fitter ones. The Rezzies aren't much better. They're ready soon enough to call us if they have a problem, a blocked food disposal unit or something, but when you arrive, it's moan, moan, moan and no offer of a cup of tea, even if there's a full teapot sitting there on the table right in front of your face.

Then, of course, there's the rule book, all eight hundred and fifty pages of tiny print of it. You can't so much as blow your nose without checking whether you've done it in the right way, nostril by nostril, using the right bloody size of handkerchief. When we first arrived at the Towers, we were supposed to carry a copy with us everywhere, but enough is enough even for a put-upon bunch like us. We made a few suggestions to the Deputy Chief Caretaker about where that aforesaid rule book could be stuffed and so he spoke to the Chief Caretaker directly (forbidden to us by rule three, subsection 4b) and for once they saw the point. So we all handed back our rule books, and though we still hadn't any chance of catching up with a Wallscrawler, at least we didn't risk getting a hernia every time we went on patrol. Of course, there was a downside—because in my experience there's a downside to everything, even something that was nothing but a downside in the first place.

The Deputy Chief Caretaker was left as the only person who had a rule book, and when he told us something that was or wasn't in there, we had no come back. We had to accept what he told us. He's not a bad bloke, the Deputy Chief Caretaker, as Deputy Chief Caretakers go, but he was a stickler for rules and there was no way round it once he'd made a decision. He'd brandish that bloody book in front of you and that was that. No appeal. But the punishments were pretty mild (one less sausage for breakfast or extra shoe cleaning duty) but you never knew when and why they were coming. And by the Pool in the Sky, if the Chief Caretaker got word that you'd been breaking the rules, then you were in deep trouble. At least one Caretaker I know was never seen again after being sent for a ticking off by the Chief.

I'd like to say all this persecution brought us Caretakers together as a group. It didn't. A more miserable back-stabbing bunch of men you'd find it hard to imagine. I've said that the Rezzies were all moan, moan, moan, but they weren't much worse than a group of Caretakers sitting in the canteen. Of course, now and then somebody made a joke, or what passed for a joke, but usually it was a joke that nobody got until it had been explained and then it wasn't really worth the bother. And everything was always someone else's fault. And if it wasn't the fault of a Wallscrawler or a Rezzie, it was usually the fault of whichever unfortunate Caretaker wasn't there at the time. We have our meals together and we sleep in long stuffy dormitories together on single beds that murder your back, so perhaps that's why we were so miserable. Maybe we were meant to be miserable though that's not what it said on the ticket when we all booked into Paradise Towers. Build High for Happiness? Do me a favour.

Also, it's worse for me because I'm one of the youngest of the Caretakers. A few months older and I've been packed off to fight in the war against whoever we were fighting. Sometimes I think I'd rather have been atomised into a billion particles or whatever happened to our brave soldiers (no idea but they certainly never came back) than put up with a life like this one. No wonder I ate too much. No wonder I had to have my uniform enlarged. So I suppose I should feel lucky that there was a small group of us younger Caretakers who got on together. Well, by the standards of the rest of the miserable bunch of old geezers, to whom I was always number 112 stroke 9 subsection 7, even though I'd known them for years and since there were only a hundred or so of us, this subsection business was bloody absurd. With us younger Caretakers, we got to shortening each other's names, so everybody called me 'Sev' and my best mate, number 87 stroke 3 subsection eight was 'Eight-ee.' But I wouldn't even tell him that, in my head, I had a special secret name. Stan. Well, you need to feel you're special in some way, don't you, even if you're not?

Our lives were dull and monotonous and I don't think I ever expected that to change. But it did. And it came about like this. As I said, the Rezzies were always on the talkiphone to the Deputy Chief Caretaker, complaining about something or other and the rule book dictated that we had to go and try and sort out the problem, even though we'd get no thanks for it and chances were that whatever component was needed to solve the problem we'd run out of years ago. So when the Deputy Chief Caretaker instructed me to go to Flat 333 Potassium Street to sort out some moaning Rezzie's problem with her heating, I fully expected I'd been sent on a fruitless errand with the added bonus of having to listen to some dreary old biddy moaning on about the old days and how lovely the Towers used to be and if only we Caretakers did our job properly, it didn't have to be like this. But what was the point in protesting? I went.

Flat 333 Potassium Street had a front door like any other front door in the whole of the Towers, though the door knocker did look as if it had been polished within living memory. So I knocked and the door opened.

'Hello,' she said and she actually smiled. Shock number one. I nearly had a heart attack. 'How kind of you to come, Caretaker number 112 stroke 9 subsection 7.' Shock number two. She'd actually bothered to remember the name of the caretaker who was coming to see her. 'Do come in and have a cup of tea.' Shock number three. She was offering me a cup of tea.

It all seemed too good to be true. I thought it might be some sort of a trap even, but I recovered from my shock and entered. And I have to say it was the lightest, brightest Rezzie apartment I've ever seen. Normally their apartments were stuffed full of rubbish, bits of ornaments, photos of cats, horrible vases with plastic flowers in them. But this apartment was different. Just a few flowers nicely arranged in a simple vase. A tea pot and two cups on the table, just simple white, no horrible squirly red, green and blue flower patterns all over it. The whole apartment was like that from what I could see. No clutter, no piles of horrible coloured cushions all over the furniture. No little rugs on the floor for you to trip over. Not a cat photo in sight. This, I thought, was how the flat's must have been meant to look. Bright, spacious, airy, with just the right amount of furniture but not too much. Even the kitchen area had neat stacks of spice bottles clearly labelled, not the usual clutter of jars and pots of all shapes and sizes jumbled together any old how.

'Do sit down, Caretaker number 112 stroke 9 subsection 7, and make yourself comfy.' I'd obviously been staring a bit longer than was polite at my surroundings so I sat down and, as she poured the tea, I finally registered the occupant of Flat 333 Potassium Street herself.

By the standards of the average Rezzie, she was a fine-looking woman. Sorry if that sounds mean but let's be honest, we Caretakers were a pretty unprepossessing bunch, so the bar wasn't set very high either for them or us. I'm not a good-looking man; I'm overweight and pasty-faced but by the standards of my colleagues, I'm a god. Same with her.

Well, no, I'm not being honest. She was a fine-looking woman, full stop. Not that I've had much experience of fine-looking women in the flesh, only on my Intergalactic Communicator Mark 7b Edition 17 where you could sometimes get a glimpse of a fine-looking woman in the flesh (and not very much else) if you were careful enough to do it while the Deputy Chief Caretaker wasn't around.

'I'm Dora, by the way,' she said as she pushed the sugar bowl my way.

I should have asked her name, of course, but most Rezzies would have been totally offended if I'd been so presumptuous and even filed a complaint with the Chief Caretaker's office.

'That's a nice name,' I found myself saying as I dropped far too many sugar lumps into my tea. Well, most Rezzies have horrible names like Gertrude or Tabitha or Ermentrude, so it wasn't that stupid a thing to say.

I'm not sure when I noticed that she had not only a pleasant smile and a face that went with it, but she was also, by Rezzie standards, very trim. You could tell because she was wearing some sort of exercise costume in tight dark grey material which went with the exercise bike tucked away discreetly in a far corner of the apartment just beyond the kitchen. I knew it was an exercise bike because there's one over at Caretaker Brainquarters, along with a load of other contraptions made of metal with levers and handles and weights which nobody ever used. So, she was the first person who possessed an exercise bike and actually used it. You could tell. Did I mention she was very trim? Normally Rezzies wear dresses that look like they're made out of old curtains (they usually are) and it takes a lot of material to cover whatever lies underneath (and I speak as one who had to have his uniform let out.) But Dora was different. She didn't need to cover herself in old curtain material.

'I'd no idea there were any young Caretakers,' she said as she poured herself a cup. With no sugar, I noted, but then I should have guessed that from the fact that she was, well, trim.

'Not that young,' I said, and felt myself blushing because of the way she was looking at me. I didn't even know then what blushing was (there's nothing about it in the rule book) but I felt that things were beginning to get a bit out of control.

'Usually, some horrible old man turns up with a sour face and a big fat belly so this is obviously my lucky day,' Dora replied. 'You aren't really called Caretaker number 112 stroke 9 subsection 7, are you?'

'That's my official description,' I responded, getting sweatier and sweatier. You cannot begin to understand how unlike this was to any conversation I'd ever had in my whole life.

'But what are you really called?' she insisted.

'My friends call me Sev,' I replied, getting in a mess with the sugar tongs.

'Then I shall call you Sev,' she announced. 'But I don't really believe that deep down that's your real name.'

She had a look in her eye like I'd never seen in anybody's eye before. I wasn't blushing any more, but my heart was pounding.

'Well?' she said, knowing I would answer.

'Stan,' I said.

'What a lovely name. Stan.' She rolled it round her mouth as if she was savouring some delicious drink. 'Stan and Dora has a certain ring, don't you think?'

The rule book was suddenly present in my brain. I couldn't recall the page or the subsection of the rule book but I felt pretty certain that we weren't playing by it. It was time to get down to business.

'Dora,' I said, 'you've lodged a complaint—number 34573—about the state of your heating system. We value your input and we will respond as soon as is possible. Which is now. So perhaps you would like to show me the heating problem you had communicated with us about.'

'You know what?' she said. 'It's the oddest thing. My heating problem went away the moment you arrived.'

Of course, there wasn't anybody I could confide in, but then a big part of me enjoyed having a secret. There they all were moaning over their teacups and I used to think, 'You wouldn't be so miserable if you could do what I'm doing.'

Not that it was easy. Dora would suggest that Caretaker number 112 stroke 9 subsection 7 had been particularly helpful and she'd enjoyed the service he provided, but she couldn't do that every time because alarm bells might have sounded. On the other hand, she was well-known as a regular complainer so anybody who could stop her complaining all the time was regarded favourably. Every older, fatter caretaker who went to Flat 333 got a flea in his ear and a complaint form completed from the lovely Dora.

The difference knowing Dora made to my life was incalculable. There was a spring in my step, and on a couple of occasions I nearly caught a Wallscrawler who was cheeking me, which surprised her almost as much as it surprised me. A large part of me—the part labelled Stan—wanted to feel free to knock on her door whenever I wanted to, but the rest of me knew I had to wait for the opportunities the system provided and make the most of them when they occurred. And Dora was the same. Her neighbours were nosy (aren't all Rezzies?) so we had to be careful and be thankful the Great Architect has provided excellent sound-proofing.

It might have gone on forever, except that nothing does, does it? My chum Eight-ee guessed there was something going on; he'd have been daft not to. So he started asking questions. Well, of course, I didn't tell him everything right away but gradually he got the point. And he made a suggestion that seemed good at the time. Why didn't he go and visit Flat 333 every now and then when she makes a complaint? That would make it all seem less suspicious to the Deputy Chief Caretaker, and she wouldn't have to pretend with me because I'm your friend.

Well, as I've said, it seemed a good idea at the time. Dora always told me what a nice young man Eight-ee was and how he always spoke well of me.

Don't ask me when I worked out what was really going on. I could tell that Dora wasn't that excited to see me now, but then the novelty had gone for me too. Not that I ever wanted to stop.

But then one day I was walking down Potassium Street by Dora's flat. Nothing special about that. I was on Rule 37 Subsection Four Surveillance Walkabout Duty. I hadn't heard from her for a few days but I thought she was being discreet because she'd been complaining about her waste disposal unit so often that it was beginning to be noticed.

The door opened and guess who came out? You don't need to guess. It was my best mate, Eight-ee, looking shifty but with no idea that I was outside. The stupid bastard had gone there without even waiting for Dora to make another complaint about the heating system.

Of course, it didn't end well. Our punch-up was registered on every surveillance camera in the whole of the Towers. We were summoned before the Chief and I thought we were going to die. Let's be honest, Eight-ee deserved some sort of punishment, but even I didn't wish the worst of the rule book on him. Let alone on myself. Luckily during the course of the punch-up we'd ended up outside Flat 337 where a very, very elderly Rezzie lived with her seventeen cats, so they couldn't pin much on Dora. And honestly, I'm glad. She changed my life. She changed Eight-ee's life. All credit to Dora.

But that wasn't how it seemed at the time. As I said, we were brought before the Chief Caretaker. Remember, Caretakers had been brought before the Chief Caretaker and never seen again. We knew we must have broken every rule in the rule book and we didn't expect any mercy.

The Deputy Chief Caretaker produced the original version of the rule book and handed it to the Chief. It was bound in leather and we'd all been brought up to respect, indeed venerate, this dust-covered original.

'I cannot begin to imagine how many rules have been broken in this disgraceful and unprecedented incident. Perhaps you can enlighten me, Deputy Chief Caretaker.'

He handed back the volume to the Deputy Chief Caretaker with a chilly smile which sent shivers down my spine. The Deputy Chief Caretaker started to consult the rule book.

One hour? Two hours? Five hours? I have no idea how many hours we sat there with the Deputy Chief Caretaker slowly turning the pages and reading every single word to himself half aloud. Even the Chief was getting visibly impatient.

Finally, the Deputy closed the book, having read it half-aloud end to end.

'Well?' the Chief asked, ready to burst into one of those rages we all feared.

'There's nothing there, Chief.'

'What do you mean?'

'The rule book doesn't cover the circumstances. There's no mention in the rule book of physical congress between Caretaker and Rezzie. Nor, I am relieved to say, between Caretaker and Caretaker.'

'Impossible!' the Chief exclaimed. He was clearly tempted to plough through the whole rule book for himself. But then he realised how long it would take and how much prestige he would lose in the process. It would also mean publicly questioning the wisdom of the Great Architect, who compiled the rule book in the first place. So, he made the best of a bad job, dealt out a few very minor punishments (a bit of extra latrine cleaning duty and no baked beans for a week) and ended up by saying:

'Caretaker number 112 stroke 9 subsection 7 and Caretaker number 87 stroke 3 subsection eight, after due process, it has been established that while you have behaved in a manner unbecoming in a caretaker, there is no underlying contravention of the rule book involved. Just be careful in the future.'

We were both eager to let Dora know what had happened. In fact, we went along together. What happened then is another matter. But at least we knew there was no description of it in the rule book.

Tricks and Treats

Alasdair Stuart

Martha on the 90th floor remembered everything. A photographic memory and growing up in a prepper family meant the walls of her apartment were lined with as many tins as they were books. That was how she bribed the Kangs; come to school, get a meal.

It worked. For a long time.

Even when things got bad, the Kangs remembered Martha's favourite holiday or rather, the shape of it. Every year, when the wind got especially cold and howled through Ballard Close like a lost dog, they would knock on every door, each gang united for a night, and say the words warped, but not broken, by memory.

'Tricks and treats!'

The smart residents gave them what they could. The smarter residents taught them what they knew. Because getting food for nothing was a good trick. But learning how to survive? No treat was better.

Except, perhaps, candy corn.

When Johnny Comes Marching Home

Simon Bucher-Jones

"It's Tommy This, and Tommy That, and Tommy How's Your Soul?
But it's thin red line o' heroes when the Drums begin to roll."

Kipling

He was a Johnny Come Home, for sure, in his tattered shoot-em-ups. Thin stuff to look at but tough. That went for him and his clothes. His soldier-boy gear had pulled out stiches of lost insignia bars at the shoulders hanging by a yellow thread against the dull faded blue. He was the first of a straggle of outlers, to arrive at the Towers. The first strangers. The first soldiers back from a half-forgotten war.

We'd never really expected anyone to ever come *back*. They'd abandoned us for glory or death, or something less imaginable, and their absence had grown into a natural thing. It felt almost wrong to have it broken, however slightly. But maybe it was also a hope, of a kind. A hope like a worry or a panic. It meant new things would have to happen, things we couldn't predict. Certainly, things were better now than during the Terror of the Cleaners but they were also less clear-cut, than something diced by the slicers of a megapodic cleaning robot.

We had problems that if less monstrous were no less difficult. Making new things, thinking them, was harder than just being afraid, or it was a different kind of fear.

'Johnny' – for we named him that when *his* problems became clear - came (by his own account) banging and shouting at the old under-ways, for there's almost as much of the Towers under the Earth as above, unseen on the showcase blueprints, but necessary, automatic and perpetual. Autofacs to rebuild it, mining engines to resupply them. Cess pools and skimmers and reclaiming engines. Basements below and around the Pit of Kroagnon. When unanswered at those once gleaming and now rusting grills, he had found a way in by tracing rat scratchings and waste-not-want-not lines. Then he'd been a scavenger in the walls for weeks before a Rezzy found him, drinking the drips in her bath-tub, and screamed for a Kang.

We're still too few to patrol everywhere, and patrolling and all such Caretaker-ness is being handled on a who-does-as-can, so it was another week still before we knew for sure there'd been other outlers among us, sneaking food from the myco-vats, and living like shadows. There were five in total including Johnny, unlooked for refugees we'd not high-spied, limping slowly, across a desert fused the colour of smoked glass, out of a horizon barely visible from the highest floors. The warriors had returned, hooray! Hooray, maybe.

Five soldiers out of our thousands (if they were ours, for what were the odds that the returnees would match the refugees?). Orphans from a now orphaned world. Young orphans which was strange. Why weren't they all old men? Hadn't they been fighting for twenty-five years or more? It seems time goes slower at the speed of their combats – no I don't understand that. I'm not sure they do.

I'd got to meet the five. There was Johnny himself with the drawl, that Pex had only ever imitated. There was Tommy This, and Tommy That – twin pale, shaking men, related maybe, or in a pash, so reliant on each other for so long as to grow alike. There was one that Johnny called the Unknown Soldier (as if they weren't all unknown), who was swathed in man-dages, eyes bloodshot with crusted sores through yellow tatters. There was one he called 'The Clattering Knight' with wrap-round prosthetics on her shattered legs, and a magazine-less empty gun, and a sword. No more so far. No more known about the ones who had come, for their memories were as tattered as their battle-dress-ups.

I'm Red Cross to the Reds or Cross Box to the Blues, and the new Yellows. In the Kangs, I'd been a healer – a shaman priestess – keeper of the medical relics. Between me and Under Caretaker Sub-Doctor 45 (they'd had no real Doctors since Time Start) there'd always been a guarded truce, a kind of professional courtesy. Someone had always to see to the sick and the older Rezzies. Now, someone had to see to the soldiers too.

The first issue was all of them had – to differing degrees – fog-getfulness - jamnesia. Hit by a mind-mine Sub-Doctor 45 thought, weaponised memory-loss. If so, that was permanent. If they were very lucky it might be just clamnesia – their own minds keeping back memories they didn't want to access. If so, that could be worked on, gradually.

The Tommies were often flat-atonic, hands clasped from parallel beddybyes. When their pale blue water eyes opened in their wan white faces they had the same kiddyness – half resentful of being awake. They had the same lisping accent too, not quite Johnny's. The Clattering Knight wouldn't let go of her weapons, not both at the same time. The Unknown Soldier kept his back to a wall. They all had their unique traumadies. It was too soon to say if they were improving.

Johnny was the most active – the most nearly Kang - maybe he'd been leading them? Come into the Towers first for a scout-about? When he was almost well enough, SD45 thought he ought to go see the Lie-burians.

I doubted they'd be any help, but they might shake something loose, and I offered (well was does-as-can-dictated) to prom him there. I told Johnny about where we were headed on the way.

The three Lie-burians – old as Rezzies, rule-booked as Caretakers, had always been secretive. The Lie-Bury with its haughty old visuals, and its edit-ifying docus, told us what the people who had left us here had wanted us to know and no more. The Lie-burians pumped the hearts-and-flowers, and the makey-overs, to the Rezzies' wallscreens. They fine-sliced the past to make it chewable for the Caretakers and they issued the Rulebooks. The Kangs had rejected them, mostly, save for sending for manuals when a thing broke, trafficking lightly in books of urban crimary, and slanguage, but keeping their own council. Kangs take what they need, make things anew. This I knew in my heart was why, still, Kangs were best.

Johnny told me the 'old-word' for such folk was Librarian, which made no sense. Kang words mean what they say.

Our words Lie-Bury, and Lie-burian are better. We stress the notruth in Lie-burian to remind us to take no grantedness. Words in books are words people put there. The old people did so wishing them to be read only in certain ways. Their authors are tricksters, enemies; the Kangs mistrust such. Moreso, we mistrust those who choose which books are read, who scaretake words, who mysterify. What is a Lib-arian? It sounded like a fa-word. Kangs have been no-fa from their first days.

"It just comes from the old word for book, 'Liber', in one of the dead languages: Latin probably. Librarians are just people who look after books, and a collection of books is a Library."

Johnny remembered somethings well enough, when he felt like saying. He had some non-personal, non-war memories. Language, how to tie his shoes, useful but not *useful.* Was that suspicious? Mind clear enough to show-off, not to tell-all? I couldn't weigh it. He'd won over many. The Rezzies loved to pluck at his cheeks, hug-hoping. The few Caretakers-as-was, still loved orders: they'd follow him if he asked. They'd followed anyone and anything before. The council of Kangs kept its likes for the proven. He'd got his own need-to-know though, before we got to the books. So, I taught him of the Lie-burians. I'd had more contact with them than most Kangs, for medi-texts had been needful.

"Of the three, Madame Prim – is the easymost – if her mood is not rueful. If it is she won't speak, though even then she may point out a voluble or a viddy. Proffer Andrew – is non-fic, or says so – and goes rageiful if his factoids are doubted, though often Kangs find they disagree with things said or given earlier. Still, he will always talk, too much timesome. 'Rector Sully-Ann covers fic, and runs the Towertelly for the Rezzies. Sully-Ann says self is "they". They have so much cutting-out work, they say – we think they mean they censor and block any old things about the war, about Outside. Rezzy stuff is all soppy-safe. Snipped down."

"Is it going to be worth trying to talk to the Lie-burians if they aren't prepared to speak to us or show us the truth?"

I don't know – I thought – Johnny – is it worth trying to talk to you if you aren't prepared to speak to us or show us the truth? But all I said was: "We believe in trying. Trying is brave. If they can not or will not help then we have lost nothing but today. Today is always lost by tomorrow. Take heart."

It was quite a way to the Lie-Bury on the 145th floor, particularly with lift-out and door-jam, and I did all I could to get Johnny at ease. He'd need to bestface and high-polite it, and some soldier manners aren't Tower manners. For'stance, saluting is a Caretakerness and not for Lie-burians. I tried to 'splain this.

He joked, or said as joke, that 'he couldn't see me curtsaying." I said all Kangs curt-say. We say as-is quickly without cowardly culetness or notruth, but he means a sort of weird movement, which he shows me by doing, and which is very silly.

I tell him not to do that as the Liar-burians will laugh at him. Somehow that is amusing to both of us. Perhaps he can be trusted. Maybe.

The Lie-Bury, has a red sign – and in accordance with the Council of Kangs pact – a blue one, and a yellow one in memory. It declared that the Lie-Bury was open for loans, which means we have to go in one at a time – which is custom.

Johnny finds this funny when I say it, but it is not funny – Madame Prim has a gun, and while it's an old gun and her aim is bad, she has been known to shoot at the second person to try and go in. Proffer Andrew is also *scar-castic*, and Sully-Ann gets over-excited by too many people, and wants to make them pose while they get photographs. Mostly of their clothes though they have their excitednesses. We do not know if their camera even works; we do know that Prim's gun does – or did, though it might have run out of ammunition by now.

I had forgotten this, and it is tricky. I want Johnny to talk to them, but I want – why do I want it so much? – to be there when he does. Is it because I don't trust him or because he's been my special charge? Well, mine and SD45 who doesn't count being a Caretaker-as-was with the pash of a wall-brick. I don't know, but I decide that I will risk it and make it just a joke and go in two-by-two, as they say animals do.

"Don't shoot, Madame Prim," I shout, "We are coming in two-by-two because Johnny doesn't know the Lie-Bury's ways. But he will do speaking and I will just be standby him to helpout.

"Prim's asleep, do you want her in particular? I suppose no one else is good enough for you?" This is Proffer Andrew, all drystick touchiness.

"Professor Andrew," Johnny makes a bobbing motion, which is almost like a curtsay and is very funny. I do not laugh since Proffer Andrew will take offense if I do and say it is laughing at him. Already Johnny has got his name wrong, which may cross him. But, no Proffer Andrew seems gladsome.

"Indeed, this is a pleasure. It has been a long time since I was given an appropriate amount of respect from some people."

Here Proffer Andrew glared at me, for no reason at all. Surely, he must understand I called out for Madame Prim first because of her gun? I did not set her above him, I merely did not wish Johnny nor myself to be shot.

"I've recently arrived at Paradise Towers, and I'm having trouble with my memories of outside. Its possible I and my…squad, if that's the word I'm looking for, may have been subjected to some kind of amnesiac gas, or ray."

"Or they may be traumafied," I add, "either way, we thought maybe you might have records of War-ness, or facts about the Outside, and that ifso then they might get Johnny's mind working to see them."

"Hmm, possible. I have tried to explain to the Kangs' that the war is only one teleological scenario, setting out a potential rason d'etre for our present society. It has explanatory power and serves as a post-facto occam's razor assumption for the absence of male citizens between what might be termed the ages of martial endeavour, but it is by no means certain that it is correct merely because it covers our circumstances."

I understand about half of this, but Johnny nods thoughtfully. "Are there no records then, in terms? I suppose I was hoping for something like a newsreel or a telepress that might say what we were fighting and dying for? I assure you we are, or were, dying for something. We have physical injuries as well as the loss of our memories; there is a war."

"There are injuries, which means there is a struggle, certainly, young man. But does that mean there is a war? I have one account that describes Paradise Towers as a "man-made planet" or space-station, and while that is counterfactual to our experiences now, might it not be that there was a time when it was true? If so, there is one reason why a space-station might orbit a planet for a time and then be brought to land. Can you think what it might be?"

"I can think of more than one reason." Johnny said brows furrowed with mental effort.

Furrowed is an odd old word we retain that only applies to the lines on people faces, I wonder if Johnny or Proffer Andrew know its first meaning?

Johnny ticked off ideas on his powerful fingers. "It might be that the war's theatre had changed from planet-side to orbital and one place of safety became a target zone. It might be that Paradise Towers' needed to replenish supplies of food and air. It might be that your source was a metaphor, that it was saying Paradise Towers was 'like' a 'man-maded planet' because it was self-sufficient and sealed off, and vast. It might be that it was once intended to be a space-station but the war or circumstances intervened and it's been, as it were, on the launch pad for all its history. Its foolish to think there's only one possible reason for things, wouldn't you say Professor?"

"Bravo, well you are a clear thinker for a military man, especially one with amnesia. You're right of course I have a favoured hypothesis, but, really, I can't rule out the ones you raise. I was, however, thinking in terms of terraforming."

This was another word I didn't know, and I didn't from the sound of it think I was going to like it.

"Turning another planet into Earth?" Johnny seemed to understand it, and maybe it didn't mean making things terrifying.

"Or a ravaged Earth, back to a liveable one. A war of a kind, but a benign one. Waged against an unfeeling lifeless terrain, or a changing climate, carried out until the benefits of its long campaigns can be brought home to those who could not wage it."

Proffer Andrew annoys me. He is a creepyman. Not in a pattyknee way like some of the Caretakers would try to be with Kangs, but because he shares view of the old people that only *some* can go-do and *others* must hide and wait. Why should we not have gone, been trained to go. Rezzies too old, Caretakers too fearful, but Kangs? Kangs are brave.

"Kangs could tame world." I find myself saying.

"I'm sure they could, now" Johnny agreed, "and I don't think it can be that sort of war, Professor. We have weapons. Not tools, weapons. We have uniforms, badges."

"Weapons are cooler than tools, and a personified enemy, is an imaginable and manageable task – whereas making over a world is an overwhelming one."

"Hmm," Johnny seemed struck by that as if it was a telling argument, "and amnesia, mind-mines? What would be the point of making people forget their jobs, forget the reasons for their efforts. I can see why an enemy might want to make us forget, but not why we would."

"Well, it is only a theory. And based on only one document. There are others that suggest Paradise Towers is only one of a chain of such Towers, housing millions of people in a fortified arch of buildings – each exerting a passive defence field: a force field if you like, against the things you were sent to fight."

"Things?"

"In that account 'things', would be the term I would use yes. Such accounts see Paradise Towers as 'Last Redoubt' of humanity."

"Aliens, like Kroagnon?" I asked.

"Perhaps, If, he was an alien."

"He was a monster, a beast! He possessed the Chief Caretaker!"

"He was, certainly," Proffer Andrew said, "those things by the end, and he did indeed possess that poor weak man. In the accounts we have his mind had already snapped when he conducted the massacre of Miracle City, but whether he was an alien must I think be open to question. We have accounts, you see, in which the 21st and 22nd century had already seen several large-scale wars against forces from beyond the Earth, even though they are now so vague and so elided for reasons of safety and security, as well as the age of the records, to be virtually stories of battles fought against absences. We do not however have accounts of a 22nd century in which humanity was so at ease with aliens as to invite them to come design their homes. A human who went mad, is a more parsimonious explanation. And his name perhaps is suggestive. A Gnomon, is a set square or a mathematical knowledge. Kroa Gnomon would mean something like 'a crooked set square' or a broken architect – a nickname in a human language, rather than a set of alien sounds."

"Sully-Ann once told me," I offered, "that Kroagnon was given the right to design structures on Earth in exchange for human architects being authorised to work on other worlds."

Proffer Andrew snorted. "Sully-Ann" thinks 'changing rooms' is a hard hitting docu of Kroagnon's early life. They're as mad as you are.

"Is there anything, anything at all – definite – that you can tell us, Professor?" Johnny was sounding a little desperate now, to my ear, and the emotion counter-cut his physical strength, with a jab-sharpness that went to my heart.

"I'm sorry," Professor (as Johnny named him, and he seemed to prefer) Andrew said, 'the only thing perhaps is that, the amnesia of Paradise Towers itself, as a whole, to its own history is, moreso than any individual forgetfulness, a great and unlikely mystery. That we have so little that is fact, that I cannot even – myself - remember the exact circumstances of twenty-five years ago seems commonplace to us, being used to it, but the teaching of history is that really, while humans possibly do not learn from history, they do not easily forget it. The very last thing humans forget is a slight or a grievance or a war. There should be songs about the stupidity and horribleness of the enemy; there should be posters on the walls still demanding that recall our brave boys in the atmosphere-trenches or wherever. We ought to have been, after only twenty-five years, deriving half our culture from obsession with the conflict, and the other half from fear of it ending – instead we seemed to forget it completely. As if out of sight really was out of mind. A thousand years might do it, but not twenty-five!"

"I wonder, Professor." (I had decided that if we were to interact with him, we might well begin by getting his name right from now on). "We've speculated about military devices that could affect memory, but only on a small scale – SDW5 and Johnny have been toying with the idea of 'mind-mines' that could have affected five people in one strike or 'explosion', but could there have been weapons that affected memory on a massive scale? What if we've all been made to forget so much, because of mind-shelling, or a creeping bombardment of forgetfulness?"

"It would be an effective weapon," Johnny said, "you can't fight a war if you forget you're fighting a war, and you don't need to destroy an enemy people, who could be useful to you, if you can destroy their memory of being a different people."

"What's this a party?"

Sully-Ann, came out of one of the side rooms at the back of the Lie-Bury, and we saw for an instance the piles of dresses and frock coats and grey fusty caretaker uniforms that they had hoarded up inside. They were wearing a mix and match up of everything, and looked – onlysaying – frightful.

"You didn't tell me we were expecting guests Andrew, I would have put film in my camera. I'll never finish my pictoral history of Paradise Towers' Fabshion, if I don't get to document each aspect of its tribal diaspora in real time."

"Johnny isn't from the Towers," I said hurriedly. I was hoping to head off Sully-Ann's 'thusiasm for interactive photog which can be trying when progress is being sought on a real problem. "He's a returned combatant. We're trying to get his memory working, so that we can help him – but it seems we ourselves aren't much better. Although I was only four or five when we all came to the Towers, so I'm not sure I can be blamed for not remembering the details."

"Yes, that was horrible," Sully-Ann said. "A dreadful policy, though you can see why they thought if necessary if you'd learned about the earlier wars. They split people up so much to try to prevent what you'd call wipeouts. There was an awful danger that a whole culture or a whole history would go up in one weapon-strike: like friendship or village-battalions in the First Mechanised War. This building and others were filled deliberately with individuals: people from disparate families with as few genetic relationships in place as possible. It was also a long-term tactic so that if only a single building archology survived the genepool would be as non-familial as possible."

"But I have family!" I stuttered.

"You have your Kang-circle, dear, and the Caretakers had their Orders, and the Rezzies well they were best suited by the policy – for they often had an old, if non-familial, friend who could accompany them – but I'm afraid you didn't have a family in the pre-Towers' sense. Where's the Rezzy who was your grandmother, hmm? Where are the Uncles and Aunts? The Kang was your sisterhood, but it was a sisterhood without any actual sisters. That couldn't have happened by accident, indeed it would have required considerable social engineering – brutal social engineering to achieve it. People must have fought to live with their kin, well some of them anyway, during the removals to the Towers. Are you sure you wouldn't let me to get a photograph or two? This Johnny is a new type, considering the Towers' recent demographics."

"New?" I considered Johnny. He was certainly well built, whereas the caretakers were either older or scrawnier. Johnny was as well-muscled and as fit as a Kang. But he was a man as the caretakers were. What was Sully-Ann getting at?

"Yes, oh excuse me – this might be a generational thing. He is of a different skin colour to most of the Tower's residents."

I looked at Johnny again. It was true his skin was very dark, but I'd simply assumed young men, strong young men, might look like that. Why not? Some among the Kangs have such skin and we think it beautiful. The only youngish man I had ever known before the soldier's return, Pex, had had lighter skin like most, but then he had been an oddity, and I had had no reason to think of him as the template for all men. Considered straight on, Johnny really was very attractive, but it was hard to think of him as odd.

I was thinking that, instead of paying proper attention to my surroundings when Madame Prim shot him. She must have just woken up, for I got a glimpse of pink night-dress in the flash of the gun.

"East bloc!" She screamed, and her hand, thank the Unalive Kangs who went before us, shook as she fired. The muzzle-flash stung my eyes, and the noise following her shout, deafened me. Still, I thought I saw that the shot had only ripped the flesh of Johnny's arm. Then Sully-Ann brought an old Caretaker baton down on Madame Prim's gun hand, and knocked the still smoking weapon away. And then the two lie-burians were tusselling on the floor.

"Quick," I shouted – bring what medicines you have."

"Don't treat him," Prim shouted, "He's one of them. He must be a spy. Here to soften us up for attack." Sully-Ann sat on her, and her voice muffled below audibility for a moment in the turn of the scuffle.

I looked back and forth from Prim to Johnny. She looked the wilder and more dangerous, even partly pinned under an old photographer. He looked terrified. My ears were still ringing and her voice and mine were whispers, but despite the droning-boom 'Rector Sully-Ann and the Professor must have made some sense out of it all. Sully-Ann started tying Prim up with Kang Scarves, and Professor Andrew brought me a grey box with the Red Cross sign from which I get my name.

"I'm sorry about Prim," he mouthed (probably shouted, but it reached me, almost, as mime), "She's always taken the war very seriously, unlike me and Sully, she had children you see. People who had to go fight, if it was a fight. She remembers no more of the facts than we do, but she remembers the hurt of it a good deal more."

"What's East Bloc?" I ask, while my hands move without conscious thought binding a wound – that just by chance - is only a surface burn and tear.

"Again, it's vague. We have some records of a period of international tension of almost war, between two types or groups of human ideologies. Each convinced of its own rightness, each tending to the inclusion of certain countries or certain cultural types. Not invariably, there's nothing to say for certain that a specific darker skinned man would be in East Bloc or a specific lighter skinned one in West, but – if like Madame Prim, you hadn't seen anyone like Johnny for twenty-five years, well…"

He sighed. "It's no excuse, but it's a sort of explanation.

"You idiots!" Prim was shouting, and almost in tears, "He's wearing a bloody East Bloc uniform. Blue with yellow trim! And he's removed the insignia deliberately. I don't care what he looks like, he's dressed like one of them! I've worked with you for twenty-five years don't treat me as if I'm suddenly a massive racist."

"We're treating you like a massive idiot, because you're acting like one!" Sully-Ann panted.

Johnny was sobbing too. "I scavenged the clothes from a body, my own were worse still – I took the symbols off because I didn't know what they were and they frightened me. But I'd done the same with my own rags before that. Don't you understand I don't *remember.* None of us do. We might have been 'East Bloc' whatever that is. But we aren't *East Bloc* any more than Paradise Towers, is West Bloc any more, if it was at the start. We have no loyalty to masters or a cause you can't see. We're only trying to find somewhere to live and be at peace."

"That," said Sully-Ann – "Is fair enough as far as I'm concerned. Prim – if we let you up will you talk this out? I'm not going to have any more fighting in the library, we've got irreplaceable items here. Who knows where your bullet went – if its broken anything in the collection I shall be extremely cross!"

"So, er tea – anyone?" Professor Andrew chimed in. "One thing West and East Bloc agreed on according to the few legends and accounts we have, was the importance of a good brew up!"

It was a tense and strained tea-party. Such rituals are more Rezzy than Kang, but we have learned to sit through them smiling during negotiations. Prim was red-faced but wasn't going to say she was sorry. Instead, she blustered and justified herself with every sentence. Johnny was more shaken that might have been expected in a soldier, but then he'd thought himself safe in the Towers. Andrew and Sully-Ann were at odds with a colleague, anxious to reclaim her, and yet keener to learn as much as possible of Johnny, and I?

I was realising that Johnny made my heart pound faster, and that when I had thought I might lose him – I had felt worrysick. I have never pashed as some do, and laughed a little – though I hope with kindliness – as those who did, but if this was pashing then it was…it was glorious. I put my hand on Johnny's leg under the table and gave it a little squeeze. Meaning, I said to myself, to reassure him that I was on his side, but it was to feel the warmth of him, and I knew it. Maybe he could feel the same. In time.

A squeaking buzz from an intercom wall-speaker – the caretakers had been working hard, to get them functioning again – interrupted my dreamydaying. I recognised the high-pitched voice of SD45, "Red Cross Box? Can you hear me, we've got a human resource problem. I need Johnny to talk to the Clattering Knight – she's gone Cleaner. She's holed up in the pharm, and brewing something up out of the medi-stuff and won't come out. I don't understand what's wrong and she won't talk to me. It turns out her gun's still got charge – must have been bi-functional - she's melted the doorlocks."

I had pressed up to the intercom, to answer and now Johnny joining me brought his mouth close to mine just off the black surface of the comm-box. His breath was warm. I took a step back all blushful, but thank the Unalive his intent was on SD45's words.

"Can she hear me?"

"I believe so, I've got the intercom in the pharm, patched into this – if she isn't so angry as to burn it out with her gun."

I groaned, that was SD45 all over. A good doctor but prone to blurt out his every thought even when it might be disastrous. She might well burn out the intercom *now*. But, surprisingly perhaps, she didn't. Instead, her voice came through – deep and scared.

"Johnny? I have to have something for the pain, they don't understand. I'm dying."

"You're not dying – you've had these attacks before, try to remember, it's the interfaces between your cybernetics and your flesh – they can go wrong and press on the nerve endings. It will pass, remember that. You will be ok."

"But it hurts so much, now. I just want it to stop." Her voice, pleading grew higher – more Kang-like.

I had a sudden suspicion, that I hated myself for. I'd forgotten in the depth of her voice, in her mechanised state, that the Clattering Knight was a woman. How close had she and Johnny been? And that might mean she was definitely East Bloc – after all, our patriarchy hadn't sent women to fight, had they? All the children left in the Towers had been women.

"We're coming back, as quickly as we can – try to hold on. Pax."

She had a name and he remembered it. My Johnny who couldn't remember his own.

"Talk to her," he took the handphone piece off the wall-comm, "keep talking as we go."

"Me? How can I help, you know her!"

"I don't. I know a name, well two names. Hers and her brother's. And I've heard you use that."

I must have been oh-mouthing like a Rezzy bowl-fish – trying to make sense of this.

"Pex," he said, urgently. "She's his sister – she went, he stayed. That's all I know of her story, all she remembered. A brother who'd always wanted to be strong, a sister who had always wanted peace – but it was the sister who took her brother's place when the war actually came, because real fear can break even the greatest strength, but peace is worth fighting for. She wasn't ready to tell anyone, but hell – she can only hate me – make her see she's home, even if the rest of us aren't. She's the one from here, or the one who would have been shipped here – if you insist on getting the technicalities right. They both got orders, draft and transhipment. He was scared, she was eager. Eager or dutiful, I don't know."

"Pax," I said, "Pex helped save us all. If you saved him from the war, you helped save us all. We won't forget him, and you are home. The Towers need heroes, and we have then, but we need information too. We need to know the truths that were kept from us, and the pains we draft-dodged. We need you all as witnesses, so that nothing like this ever happens again."

There was sobbing down the comms, and a sound that was half-electric crackle and half scream. Was she shooting through walls? Had something mort-circuited?

"SD45 is down", a Kang's voice shouted – one of the youngers. Behind her (or quieter which I intuit as behind in my headspace) a caretaker starts reciting rules for emergency fire-ups. "Rule 41 b) If fire is electrical, acquire, requisition, or obtain a type 7KP CO2 CANNISTER extinguisher. 41 c) if a 7KPCO2C is unavailable, a dry powder 9LAMONOAMPHO may be substituted following completion of a MISEQ78-K form." By this time, we are kicking a jammed-lift door open and I am doing my best to jump-start it. This can work for a couple of floors and will save us steps.

Pax's voice bass-thrums through the comm. "I said stay back! You shouldn't have got the door open. I don't want to hurt any of my brother's friends – I just want to shut down, to have the pain stilled, to be unalive. Can't you understand that? I had hope of him being here, and then he wasn't, and I don't even remember him – not properly. I don't want saving."

The lift lights flick as we head to the Resty-Rooms – which is old words for the medicals.

Johnny tries: "Don't you remember saving me, Pax? From the snappers in the blind trench?"

"Yes, I remember, but that was war. I had people to protect, and there were things I could kill. Now I'm not fully a person and I never will be, and you'll find other people to be with. People who will be better for you. People who aren't patchworked-up."

"That," Johnny said, "Doesn't matter."

I could tell he was trying to believe it, and I willed for him to get his voice so that it rang with certainty, but if he wasn't quite fooling me, then there wasn't much hope she'd buy it."

I snatched the comm-piece out of his hand. "Red Cross Box here, talk to me. No, not you – if you're going to die you can wait while I talk to my friend. Someone put SD45 on. I want to know if he's badly hurt." Brutal I know, but I had to try coming at things a different way, for all our sakes.

"Red Cross Box?" SD45 sounds stilted on a good-day, and now his voice goes like a slow sound on a half-speed joke-vid.

"You okay, my dear?"

"Covered in corrosive, monoammonium phosphate, but not actually on fire, RCB. Of course, I am now pale yellow, perhaps I could join the fresh start of the yellow Kangs!" This is SD45's idea of a joke, as is calling me RCB.

"You care…about him?" This is Pax.

"He's my colleague and my friend," I snap, "and until you stop being so sorry for yourself and come out and calm down, he's going to be standing there until his paint finishes peeling off!"

"You see, how it is here," Johnny tried, and he'd – thank the Great Kangs – understood what I was trick-shotting for. "Caretaker or Rezzy, Kang, or individual like your brother, it doesn't matter. Whole human or part human, or Under-Caretaker Sub-Doctor Robot 45. What matters is we help each other. We care for each other."

"We have a lot to rediscover together," I add, "History and truth, and pains we aren't going to wish away or deny, but we don't have to rediscover hate for any of us. We don't care if you were enemies, or if you've got metal legs. We don't care if you were East-Bloc to our West or vica versa. You're new people to us, all of you, and worth the world and everything in it. Please, please don't die."

Which Paradise Towers, being what is it, was when the lift jammed again and the comms-piece stopped relaying a signal.

So that was a while ago, and with things being as they are until we can find more people we're making accomodations to the circumstances. The Lie-burians tells us that poly-relationships were perfectly proper in the old days, and Pax, Johnny and I are making the best of it. The Tommy's seem happy enough together but are assisting (as will Johnny, I'll make sure of that) in donations to baby-banking, and even the as yet unbandaged Unknown Soldier has several admirers.

Would I have preferred having him just mine? Maybe. Maybe not. Ask me after an age. But while two is company, I have always believed Kangs are best.

Reclaiming Kroagnon

James Cooray-Smith

'Take Me Down To Paradise Towers': Reclaiming Kroagnon: Democratic accountability and the Defence of the Past by Dr T E Hamster, Santa Diana University, (Olympus Mons Campus)

This article first appeared in the Journal of Presentism and Transtemporal Mendacity

Kroagnon, it seems, will not fall. Pressure from various influential groups posing as grass roots initiatives has been unsuccessful, and the statue of the Great Architect installed at the opening gates of Miracle City will not be pulled down. In their virtuous stampede to banish from public spaces the spectre of a man they view (wholly without compelling evidence) as a grievous criminal, these members of a highly influential network of interconnected groups had forgotten one thing: the people.

Miracle City was Kroganon's masterpiece. In keeping with the strong egalitarian principles the historical record demonstrates this most defamed of artists to have had, Miracle City's Residents' Association was required to rubber stamp any change to infrastructure. Quite why those who pompously style themselves the 'Kroagnon Must Fall Committee' felt that as substantial a change as the removal of a sixty storey statue of Flidorian Gold would be able to bypass such a rule is a mystery.

I jest, of course. It is no mystery at all. They felt entitled to bypass the freeholders, leaseholders and tenants of Miracle City because such people do not believe in democratic accountability. That an adjudicator's decision was needed to legally force the 'Kroagnon Must Fall Committee to either gain the explicit consent of Miracle City's residents or abandon their plans to destroy a magnificent piece of public art speaks volumes about the nature of their movement.

Equally loud is the fact that not one single resident of Miracle City voted in favour of the removal of Kroagnon's statue. Not one. That Miracle City has no inhabitants, because of the series of lethal accidents which befell anyone who ever walked into the building, is entirely irrelevant. Democracy is not the 'legal technicality' it was described as being by Bin Liner of the Red Kang Brigade. To claim that it is, is the kind of intellectually empty solipsism one has come to expect from the self identified 'Ice Hot', and their assertions in favour of what they call 'equality'.

The campaign against Kroagnon's statue has nothing to do with equality as anyone familiar with a dictionary might understand it. It is about purging the present of anything that might conceivably make anyone uncomfortable. Even if their own reasons for feeling so are meaningless. Thank goodness there was a group of intellectuals, such as myself, prepared to stand up and argue back against the baying mob who are trying to rewrite the history not just of Kroagnon, the Great Architect, but of the human race. In truth, the Ice Hot knew full well that they couldn't remove the statue. In appealing the decision, and signing themselves up for an expensive legal battle that they know they can't win, they are making a classic virtue-play; their intention is not to win, it is just to show how Ice Hot they are.

Many of us raised alarm bells more than a decade ago, when Bin Liner and her wife began renaming areas of Paradise Towers named by the Great Architect, reconfiguring them around events deemed of historical significance by those who run the Towers. (I said at the time that 'These people who want to change history would be better served trying to make some history of their own, instead of trying to abolish the ones we already have.') The lovingly named Fountain of Happiness Square became Pex Lives! Plaza, despite the ugly syntax of that construction. We were told to regard this not as historical revisionism, and possible occultism, but instead the 'reclaiming' of the Towers by its residents from Kroagnon, seen by the revisionists as the oppressor of the residents of Paradise Towers. Rather than as the man who provided their housing.

Of course, not all residents of Paradise Towers are created equal in the eyes of Red Kangs. Indeed, they long ago succeeded in making 'Okay, Rezzie' a scattershot term of abuse. But, as responsible historians, we should look again at the residents, and the accusations of cannibalism made against a whole generation of women who lived in the Towers, most of whom are conveniently too dead to defend themselves against what further evidence may well demonstrate to be an unfounded slur. But unfounded slurs are the stock in trade of the Ice Hot. They do not care for a scrupulous account of the human race's colonial past. Their only interest is in pillaging it for present political advantage, and in calling into question the validity of human colonisation of space itself.

Because the warnings of myself and others were not heeded in good time, there is now an Ice Hot vanguard in academia. Led by the likes of my former departmental colleague, Megali Scoblow, and the author of *The Zen Military* (whose name I am unable to mention due to pending litigation), who make use of time and resources allocated by both the state and the market for the education of the next generation of human children to instead questions the morals, motivations and accomplishments of their ancestors. This looks like badly misplaced priorities from these institutions. Instead of pandering to the Ice Hot, they should be focused on their important day jobs.

I have lost count of the number of purportedly academic conferences I have attended where, for example, junior, and often non-human colleagues, have argued that Claudio Tardelli deliberately made art that damaged the material universe. But now academics feel compelled, even entitled, to believe that such outre claims should be used to direct public policy. During recent public discussions of the final report issued by the

Adjudicators' Commission on Intrahuman Economic Disparities, its chief author and chairman, Adjudicator General Sir Nigel N Nigel-Nigel, forcefully complained that it had been vilely misrepresented as the glorification of child abuse.

He was responding to comments made on the day of publication by Scoblow, who had demanded that the government urgently explain how they came to publish content which glorifies child abuse and immediately disassociate themselves from these remarks. What was the basis for Scoblow's shocking accusation? A single, innocent sentence in the foreword proposing that students—such as those with whose education she is personally entrusted—be taught not only about how the children of Paradise Towers suffered during the years of its discommunication from human space, but also about why it was felt necessary to cease communication in the first place. Of course, Professor Scoblow does not believe that Nigel-Nigel condones the abandonment of children. She is simply looking for a headline, and as ever, attempting to blame humans for what happens to humans. That humanity was fighting a war against non-human interests in those years is not relevant. (It needs to be said, although some will object to it, that Professor Scoblow is herself not human.)

To date, this well-funded coalition of vested, anti-human interests has, with its aggressive zeal, succeeded in overawing a majority who know too little history to contradict them. But the problem with running out ahead of the evidence is that it leaves you exposed. Therein lies the hope for an effective resistance. The more that the facts are soberly presented in all their plausible complexity, the more naked they will become. As I am about to demonstrate, soon the Ice Hot will find themselves suddenly very cold indeed!

So are the supporters of the Red Kangs correct? Have they got their history right? Was Kroagnon diabolical? The case against him is this:

that he held all life in contempt and that he sought to exterminate all living things within Paradise Towers. That this demonstrates that the accidents which made Miracle City literally uninhabitable were not accidents at all, but a deliberate series of murders orchestrated by Kroagnon. Circular logic is then applied to make what happened at Miracle City prefigured the massacre at Paradise Towers, rendering it part of a pattern of murderous behaviour on Kroagnon's part. In short, that Kroagnon was Paradise Towers' Hitler.

The supporting evidence is encapsulated in a quotation deployed by Ice Hot campaigners:

'Search hard, my Cleaners, search hard. Bring them all out! All the nasty human beings! The Caretakers, the Residents, the Kangs, all of them! We'll be back to collect the rubbish later.'

But the bald fact is, there is no proof that Kroagnon was involved in the massacres (if massacres they truly were) at either Miracle City or Paradise Towers. What transpired at Paradise Towers did so decades after Kroagnon's presumed death. That is forgotten now, so keen are we to accuse the man of murder. It was, at the time, a surprise to be told that Kroagnon had secreted himself in Paradise Towers shortly before it lost contact with the rest of human space, and in his splendid isolation gone mad.

It seems wholly remarkable now that, following Paradise Towers' re-discovery by Captain Cook, the accounts (provided by a mere handful of 'witnesses') of what had happened there during the preceding decades were accepted so uncritically. Oh! How the historians of the day erred in their embrace of the tainted testimony of a small group of young women with admitted criminal pasts. 'I believe her,' became a common phrase, its use pioneered by Megali Scoblow. The supposed trauma suffered by that generation, who were raised in the most luxurious and magnificently designed housing project of all time, their every need catered to by cleaning robots and self-replenishing food dispensers, was deployed to attack the motives of anyone who questioned their recall.

When security camera footage from Paradise Towers was finally handed over to an independent panel of historians it did, as the United Rainbow Kang Flag claimed, demonstrate that the floor by floor massacre at Paradise Towers did take place. (Full disclosure: I was its chairman and, I confess, I was amongst those historians who doubted the historicity of the event.) Yet it also demonstrated that the man ordering the cleaners to wipe out the humans of the Towers was the Chief Caretaker of Paradise Towers and not Kroagnon at all. The quotes from 'Kroagnon' which so-called historians and overt campaigners had accepted uncritically were spoken by someone else entirely and on camera! A someone else who had had the summary execution of Kroagnon, should he return to Paradise Towers, written into the Caretakers' Rulebook. A book which was never to be questioned.

So, it is not that Kroagnon's culpability for the death toll at Paradise Towers is in question. It's that his presence is not demonstrable, and that there is an alternative, and more credible, candidate, who himself can be shown to have been an enemy of the Great Architect. Acceptance of Kroagnon having any role at all in the Paradise Towers Massacre involves acquiescing to an unevidenced claim by Drinking Fountain, latterly the CEO of Blue Kang Travel. She made, and then under pressure retracted, the frankly bizarre allegation that Kroagnon had achieved something she called 'corpoelectroscopy' and possessed the body of the by then late Chief Caretaker! (Corpoelectroscopy is not a word, unless it is one that Drinking Fountain made up.)

It is time that someone dares to ask why the Ice Hot, a movement that seems stridently anti-human, or at least anti human civilisation, should be so concerned with the fates of the people within Paradise Towers, other than because some of their own members number amongst them. The wide ranging cultural influence of the Ice Hot is only possible because of how such groups are funded. We mere mortals, of course, do not know how that is. But they always seem to be underwritten not by actual humans. Or if by humans, then not by humans who have any links to Earth. Which is essentially the same thing. Was whatever truly happened in Paradise Towers in those years something which severed the loyalties those left behind should naturally have had to their own species? Are the people who were welcomed back into human civilisation when Paradise Towers was rediscovered really still people at all?

There may be simpler, if no less sinister, explanations. Drinking Fountain was, as she later acknowledged, personally responsible for the 'Pex Lives!' wallscrawl which began that particular cult. She asks us now to excuse that as a youthful indiscretion. The kind of indiscretion that she would not permit us forgive the likes of her rescuer, Captain Cook. Once the most famous of intergalactic explorers, he has been reconfigured by the Ice Hot as a mere tourist, visiting places which, in the views of the Ice Hot, did not need discovering, because their inhabitants were already aware of them! There's worse to come. The Captain's bravery at the Groz Valley of Melogothon has been caricatured by Professor Scoblow in the pages of this very journal as murderous on a scale comparable with the alien occupation of the Captain's home planet, begun in 2164! (Why we should listen to the opinions of species of non-Earth origin on human history is quite beyond your present author; I submit this opinion in the full knowledge some will label it 'racist'. While noting that the Kangs themselves choose to be segregated by self-identified colour.)

The smears of Captain Cook, like those on Kroagnon, work by cynically attacking the man's strengths rather than his weaknesses, leaving those who would defend their honour unsure how to respond. The werewolf Mags, saved by the Captain from a murderous mob on her own planet, and whom some biographers have seen as the muse of the Captain's later life, is reconfigured by the mean-spirited as a mere 'specimen' or a hostage. Whisper it, a slave. Their evidence? The Captain is quoted as saying 'Everything is a specimen of something!' in relation to Mags. Perhaps he did. But 'Everything is a specimen of something!' is an inherently egalitarian phrase. The first word means the Captain must have included himself in his description, but no amount of dishonesty is beneath equality activists whose position is, in truth, anti-human. Alone amongst space-faring species, homo sapiens have little to be ashamed of in their twenty first century histories. For those humans who have become anti-human, this is simply too much. Architects and explorers must be held to account for the great criminals they are! And if building things and finding things cannot be made a crime, we must instead concentrate on the suffering and oppression of those who were oerced into building. Assuming we can make them up fast enough.

Anti-human 'decolonising' and 'equality' activists typically prefer noise to nuance. In their zeal to press home a political point, they also run far out ahead of the historical evidence. We are burning our cultural inheritance. There genuinely is a crisis of Human civilization if even Kroagnon can be made into a monster. This at times looks like the suicide of humankind. Following some high-profile character assassinations, it's high time we reassessed him as a brilliant self-made outsider who overcame humble beginnings, a hostile establishment and his own mental health to become The Great Architect.

Kroagnon was once a name that humans wrote and said with pride. They should do so again

Pex Strikes!

Written by

Voga Keplis

[NOTE TO PRODUCER: I know you still don't believe me but this is all true. Apart from the bits that aren't. You know how it is.

RE: 'THAT' SCENE - I've removed the love scene as requested but I resent compromising my artistic vision just because it wouldn't play well with the audiences on Betalon IX - I don't care how big a market they are!]

INT. PARADISE TOWERS, FOUNTAINS OF HAPPINESS SQUARE - DAY

We open on a busy square in Paradise Towers. Rezzies and Caretakers go about their day, chatting and laughing...

REZZIE #1
Another day in Paradise!

REZZIE #2
Oh yes duck. Isn't it peaceful?

BOOM! The wall explodes! Screams in the crowd as a giant MUTANT RAT scurries from the hole in the wall. Rezzies scatter, the Caretakers are quickly over run.

A lone figure emerges from the smoking hole...

REZZIE #1
Oh my, it's...

CUT TO: Hero shot. The smoke clears revealing PEX. He's young, athletic and ready for action.

PEX
It's me Pex. I'm here to put the world of Paradise Towers to rights.

REZZIE #1
I was going to say it's all your fault,

isn't it?

Pex doesn't hear her as, with a single bound, he leaps up onto the fountain, blaster in hand. He watches. He waits. The perfect moment...

HE STRIKES! Pex dives onto the back of the mutant rat. He grabs it's ears and yanks hard. The foul creature topples, Pex holding on. They roll and tussle.

The mutant rat's tail whips at Pex. He drops his blaster! The blaster lands in front of a robot cleaner trundling into the square. The machine starts to pick up pieces of debris.

Pex is thrown clear. He rolls and in one fluid motion is back on his feet. The rat turns. They face off. The mutant creature drags it's claws on the floor.

PEX

I don't want hurt you, foul creature... But you leave me no choice!

The creatures roars as it runs towards Pex. He Pex dives at the creature and the tour wrestle. Pex grunts as he slowly pushed the creature back...

Back towards the robot cleaner and it's rotating drill attachment... With one last effort Pex pushes the creature back. It loses it's footing and falls onto the maintenance machine's deadly machinery.

The creature writhes. Pex feels a moment of pity for it.

The moment passes. The crowd has gathered around him.

PEX (CONT'D)

It's okay everyone. It won't harm you any longer.

The crowd parts for BIN LINER and her RED KANGS.

BIN LINER

It wouldn't have hurt anyone if you hadn't let it go muscle-brain!

PEX

It was trapped. Suffering!

BIN LINER

Our trap! Rotten rats have been munching up the lower levels. Too many wipe-outs. Oldsters doing nothing so we caught one.

Bin Liner pushes Pex.

BIN LINER (cont'd)

Then you ruined everything rubber neck!

A murmur in the crowd. Armed CARE TAKERS lead by the CHIEF CARE TAKER himself enter the scene.

BIN LINER (CONT'D)

Trouble now! Come on, all speed!

The Kangs disappear into the crowd. Pex gathers himself.

CHIEF CARETAKER

Pex. I should have known.

PEX

That's all right Chief. How could you have known there were Mutant Rats in Paradise Towers. Don't worry I'm here to put the world of Paradise Towers to rights.

CHIEF CARETAKER

And I'm here to put you in the detention centre! GRAB HIM!

CUT TO:

INT. SOAP DISH'S APARTMENT - DAY

A dingy apartment on the lower levels. Damp stains peel wallpaper. The floor is littered with the detritus of an impoverished life. Enter SOAP DISH, a strong but fragile, beautiful but deadly vision in yellow. She elbows the door open - the mechanism is in need of repair.

SOAP DISH
Milk Bottle? I'm home!
(grunts)
Hey! A little help?

Soap Dish squeezes through the door carrying a bag of groceries.

SOAP DISH (CONT'D)
Milk Bottle? Hey sis, where you at?

Soap Dish looks around the apartment. SUDDENLY she freezes. Time slows. The bag of groceries drops to the floor.

Tumbling from the bag, a milk bottle - it SMASHES on the ground.

Soap Dish runs to her sister, a crumpled heaped on the floor. MILK BOTTLE's skin is grey, her eyes rolled into the back of her head. She'd be beautiful if she wasn't dead.

SOAP DISH (CONT'D)
Milk Bottle! No time for games! You can't... You can't be unalive! You can't!

Soap Dish holds her sister to her. Desperately

she looks around the room. Then she sees it -

SOAP DISH (CONT'D)

No! No no no!

- the hypodermic injector. The empty vial. The sticky residue of illicit substances. Soap Dish grabs the injector.

SOAP DISH (CONT'D)

You promised! You promised you'd stop!

Soap Dish determined.

SOAP DISH (CONT'D)

I'll make them stop. Put an end once and for all.

INT. DETENTION CELL - DAY

PEX sits in the detention cell. The door slides open. The Chief Caretaker walks into the room carrying his rules and regulations book.

CHIEF CARETAKER

By rights I should throw the book at you.

The Chief Caretaker hefts the large rules and regulations book to prove he's willing to do it. [NOTE TO PRODUCER: I've seen the early props designs - I mean it, this book should be

HUGE]

PEX
No need Chief. I don't play by the rules. I know what's right.

CHIEF CARETAKER
Then you should have gone to war. Young fellah like you. Done your duty.
(under his breath)
Anywhere but here.

PEX
But chief, then there would be no one to put the world of Paradise Towers to rights.

CHIEF CARETAKER
I've told you... You will refer to me as the Chief *Caretaker*.

PEX
And I've told you... I'll always take care of Paradise Towers. That's my duty.

The Chief Caretaker grimaces.

CHIEF CARETAKER
By rights I should put you in an Article Fifteen Subsection Gamma Paragraph B incarceration...
(sighs)

but you did put an end to that creature.
(steps aside)
So this time it's just a warning.

Pex remains seated.

CHIEF CARETAKER (CONT'D)
So get out of my sight before I change my mind.

Pex bounds to his feet, giving the Chief Caretaker a hearty slap on the shoulder.

PEX
Thanks Chief, you won't regret it!

Pex marches purposefully out of the cell. The Chief Caretaker massages his temples.

CHIEF CARETAKER
I already do.

CUT TO:

INT. CARETAKER CONTROL HUB - DAY

Two caretakers enter the hub as PEX puts on his bandolier.

CARETAKER #1
Are you going to tell him?

CARETAKER #2

Why is it always me?

CARETAKER #1

You've got a way with words. He doesn't get as mad with you.

CARETAKER #2

Yeah, but normally it's small things. A leaky pipe, wallscrawl or a faulty cleaner. But this... this is big trouble!

Pex can't resist.

PEX

Big? How big? I'm great at trouble.

CARETAKER #1

Yeah. Getting into it! Why don't you clear off, eh?

Pex, dejected, gathers up his belongings and leaves the room.

CARETAKER #1 (CONT'D)

Look, we've got to tell the chief! It's a Section Nine, category A emergency. Someone is draining power from the power plant!

Around the corner: Pex is hiding, listening in. He fastens his bandolier and walks out of the control hub.

INT. BUTTER KNIFE'S APARTMENT - DAY

BUTTER KNIFE, a yellow Kang with a heart of gold, opens the door.

BUTTER KNIFE

How you do, Soap Dish?

Soap jDish wraps arms around the other Kang.

SOAP DISH

She's unalive! Milk Bottle... smashed!

Butter Knife ushers her fellow yellow Kang into the apartment.

BUTTER KNIFE

What happened?

SOAP DISH

That habit. That filthy, rotten habit it kicked her good. My little sister she's...

Soap Dish pushes Butter Knife away.

SOAP DISH (CONT'D)

It's all my fault!

BUTTER KNIFE

How that?

SOAP DISH

I should have known. Should have protected her. She was going clean.

Soap Dish crosses the room. She gathers herself.

SOAP DISH (CONT'D)

Drugs didn't come from thin air. Someone put them in her hand. Going to find them. Take them to the cleaners.

Butter Knife is uneasy.

BUTTER KNIFE

How can I help?

SOAP DISH

Won't put you in harm's way. But you listen to the whispers in the walls. Know what's what and going up in the world. You must have heard something?

BUTTER KNIFE

I don't know much. This drug, they call it Fyx. Don't know where Kangs are getting it.

(beat)

But I'll help. No to do.

Soap Dish takes off her ruck sack. She unloads the contents onto the table. The injector, the vial.

SOAP DISH

We have to find the ones responsible. Make all speed before another Kang gets wiped out.

BUTTER KNIFE

And when you find them Soap Dish? What then?

SOAP DISH

I'm gonna take them to the cleaners.

CUT TO:

INT. SECRET DRUG LABORATORY - DAY

A dingy, badly light drugs lab in the bowel of Paradise Towers. We hear the heavy thrum of machinery on the level above. LT. BRUCKHEIMER tends to the latest batch, sifting and cutting the crystal FYXAPHELETAMINE with scavenged products. He pours some into a vial with a funnel.

A door slams open and LT. SILVER storms into the laboratory. Bruckheimer jumps, spilling the batch.

SILVER

Bruckheimer you idiot!

BRUCKHEIMER

Damn it Silver, I'm trying to work.

Silver grabs his accomplice by the collar.

SILVER

It's not good enough. Stupid girls getting themselves killed. Of course! Can't expect a Kang to follow orders...

BRUCKHEIMER

There's only so much to go around. I can't replicate the original batch fast enough... having to cut it with whatever I can find.

SILVER

Sloppy. If the Chief Caretaker finds out it'll be an Appendix 3, Subsection 9 death for both of us!

(spits)

Assuming the Kangs don't get us first.

Silver lets Bruckheimer go.

SILVER (CONT'D)

Where's Gordon?

BRUCKHEIMER

Fetching more cleaner. I need it to cut the stuff. No one will notice if a few more bottles go missing.

SILVER

No more risks. No more second chances.

BRUCKHEIMER

Don't worry, one bad batch isn't going to kill us. A few tripped out junkies maybe... But this next batch is better. Going make us some good scratch. You'll see.

Silver rubs his jaw.

SILVER

I hope so. For both our sake's...

CUT TO:

INT. POWER PLANT CORRIDOR - NIGHT

The nuclear core of Paradise Towers. This is what keeps the lights on - though they're dimmer now that the Towers are in their night cycle. A steady thrum of power can be heard in an otherwise quiet, empty corridor leading to the central control hub.

CLANG! Pex kicks his way through a ventilation

grate. Athletically, he drops down into the corridor, landing in a crouch. He move towards the control, blaster in hand, ready for action...

INT. POWER PLANT CONTROL ROOM - NIGHT

With immense effort Pex forces the door open. He enters, sweeping the room with his primed weapon.

Confident that he is alone, Pex scans over the various displays and controls. He starts pressing buttons at random, hoping to find the evidence he needs.

SOAP DISH
I wouldn't do that if I were you.

Pex turns, blaster raised. Soap Dish stands behind him, her arrow gun pointed square at his head.

PEX
Why are you stealing the power?

SOAP DISH
What? Why are you dealing in poison?

PEX
I don't know what you're talking about.

SOAP DISH

You must be used to that muscle-brain.

PEX

Whatever you're up to, it ends now.

(beat)

What are you up to?

SOAP DISH

I was following someone. Someone bad.

PEX

Who?

CUT TO:

INT. SECRET DRUG LABORATORY - NIGHT

GORDON enters the laboratory, carrying a crate of cleaning products.

GORDON

Here, this should be enough.

Bruckheimer picks up a bottle of cleaner.

BRUCKHEIMER

'Do not ingest.' Well, it doesn't say anything about injecting!

SILVER

Are you sure you weren't followed?

GORDON

Of course boss.

Silver points at his surveillance screen. Pex and Soap Dish in the control hub.

SILVER

Are you sure?

CUT TO:

INT. POWER PLANT CONTROL ROOM - NIGHT

Pex and Soap Dish in a stand off.

PEX

Lower your weapon.

SOAP DISH

You first.

PEX

I will... as soon as you lower yours.

SOAP DISH

Ugh! Talking circles, getting yawny now.

A sudden grating, grinding noise. An old mechanism groaning to life. Pex and Soap Dish turn, distracted by this new danger.

PEX

More of your friends?

SOAP DISH

More of yours?

Scritches and scratches. A terrible noise. In the shadows, something moves...

Soap Dish screams as a MUTANT RAT leaps over the control desk. She fires an arrow-!

It flies true, striking the creature in the neck but not before it can claw at her clothes. A deep, horrible cut across her abdomen.

Pex grabs her as she falls. She starts convulsing.

PEX

Don't worry. I'll get us out of here.

He carries her in his arms, running out of the control room as the howls of more mutant rats echo down the corridors...

INT. SECRET DRUG LABORATORY - NIGHT

Bruckheimer watches the surveillance monitor.

BRUCKHEIMER

My rats... That's another dead.

SILVER

They scared them off. That's what they

were made for.

Silver turns to Gordon.

SILVER (CONT'D)
You lead them here. Idiot.

GORDON
This isn't my fault.

Silver puts a heavy hand on Gordon's shoulder.

SILVER
You're right. It's my fault for letting you on this little scheme...

A concealed knife shoots out of Silver's sleeve and into Gordon's chest.

SILVER (CONT'D)
...and for not killing you sooner.

FADE TO:

INT. BLANCHE'S APARTMENT - DAY

Soap Dish lies on a comfortable sofa, her wounds bandaged. She is wary - these are unfamiliar surroundings. Slowly, she tries to move, her body aches.

BLANCHE
Steady there deary.

Blanche, a doting oldster, shuffles into the room to assist her. She wears a tatty old cardigan and thin glasses on a gold chain.

BLANCHE (CONT'D)
You've been in the wars.

SOAP DISH
Who are you?

Pex enters with a tea tray loaded with teapot, cups, saucers and little sandwiches.

PEX
This is Blanche.

SOAP DISH
Rezzies don't care much for Kangs.

BLANCHE
This one does.

Soap Dish reluctantly accepts the oldsters help to sit up.

BLANCHE (CONT'D)
Cup of tea?

Blanche pours them all a nice cup of tea.

SOAP DISH
Two lumps.

Blanche smiles. Pex squats next to Soap Dish.

PEX

Blanche was a doctor in the days before. Patches me up sometimes when I get into scrapes. You can trust her.

SOAP DISH

Trust no one.

BLANCHE

Well that's a very lonely way to be. Here you go deary.

She passes a cup and saucer to Soap Dish. The young Kang eyes it suspiciously.

SOAP DISH

No poison?

BLANCHE

No poison.

Soap Dish tries to take the cup in both hands but finds it too hot. Reluctantly, she takes the saucer too. Pex watches her as she drinks.

PEX

So if you're not the one stealing power, who is?

SOAP DISH

Don't know. Don't care. I only want to find the people who dosed my sister. Find their hide-in, burn it down.

PEX

Then what were you doing in the power plant?

SOAP DISH

The Fyx, they mix it with clean-blue. I stalked someone who was stealing some. Hoped to find their hide-in but lost tracks.

BLANCHE

Did you say Fyx?

PEX

What is it Blanche?

BLANCHE

Fyxametapheladone. A very powerful pain killer. They use it on soldiers, keeps them going. Very dangerous. And now someone is giving it to these sweet girls... my goodness, they must be stopped. You must inform the Chief Caretaker at once.

PEX

He won't listen.

(to Soap Dish)

But don't worry, you're with Pex now, and I put the world of Paradise Towers to rights.

CUT TO:

INT. BUTTER KNIFE'S APARTMENT - DAY

A package wrapped in brown paper. Butter Knife unwraps the package revealing a medical case inside. She pops the latch...

REVEAL: a hypodermic injector and a vial of Fyx.

Butter Knife greedily loads the vial into the injector. She pulls back her sleeve, puts the injector to her arm. A single tear rolls down her face.

BOOM! Pex kicks through the door. He steps inside, blaster raised. Butter Knife ducks for cover.

Soap Dish follows him into the room.

SOAP DISH

Why'd you kick in?

PEX

You said she knew something about Fyx.

SOAP DISH

She was doing an ask around. Eyeing up clues. She's a friend!

She tries to help Butter Knife up.

SOAP DISH (CONT'D)

Butter Knife!

Butter Knife slowly sits up, the injector is SMASHED on the floor, the vial's contents seeping into the carpet.

BUTTER KNIFE

No! No no no! Need my fyx. Need it bad!

Soap Dish grabs Butter Knife and shakes her.

SOAP DISH

You told untruths! Got Milk Bottle smashed. It was you! Always you!

BUTTER KNIFE

Didn't think she'd... Just want to get out of my brainbox.

(sobs)

Broken. Everything's broken.

PEX

But taking Fyx doesn't fix anything. Don't you see?

BUTTER KNIFE

I'm sorry. I'm so sorry.

SOAP DISH

My little sister is unalive because of you!

Pex grabs Soap Dish before she can hit Butter Knife. She wrestles free of his grip.

PEX

Hey, go easy on her okay? Can't you see she's hurting?

SOAP DISH

Only other people!

PEX

She didn't create Fyx. She's a victim too. The ones behind this... Get angry with them!

SOAP DISH

But how? What to do? Only dead ends everywhere we turn!

A silence settles over the room. Pex doesn't have an answer. Then, meekly:

BUTTER KNIFE

I can help...

INT. VENDING MACHINES - DAY

A robot cleaner rolls towards a vending machine.

BUTTER KNIFE (V.O.)
I don't know who they are but they use one of the cleaners to drop.

The robot cleaner opens up the side of machine with it's pincer arm. The pincer arm reaches into the bin behind the robot cleaner and pulls out a PACKAGE WRAPPED IN BROWN PAPER.

BUTTER KNIFE (V.O.) (CONT'D)
Quiet footing, follow the cleaner. Find the fixers.

The cleaner deposits the package inside the vending machine, closes the side panel and trundles away.

From the shadows, Pex rolls into the corridor. Soap Dish emerges moments later... Pex comes up on one knee, surveying the area with his blaster.

PEX
(whispers)
Let's go!

Quickly and quietly they stalk after the

Cleaner.

INT. ANOTHER CORRIDOR - DAY

Pex and Soap Dish follow the Cleaner. It suddenly stops and turns...!

Pex and Soap Dish duck into a doorway. There is little space between them.

PEX

That was close.

SOAP DISH

Too close.

They look into each other's eyes. An electric spark of tension.

PEX

Very close...

He moves towards her. Soap Dish ducks her head into the corridor.

SOAP DISH

Gone.

They suddenly step out into the corridor.

SOAP DISH (CONT'D)

Which way?

PEX

Follow the smell...

[NOTE TO PRODUCER: Look, I know what you said about getting this past censors on Betalon IX but we need *some* romantic tension. People need characters they can invest in!]

INT. DEAD END SQUARE - DAY

Pex and Soap Dish round the corner into a small park. Once a square team with life... now a dead end.

The robot cleaner waits for them.

WHIRR. Its blades come to life. Its deadly pincers snap.

PEX

I smell... a rat!

They turn suddenly. TWO MUTANT RATS corner them.

SOAP DISH

Rat trap!

PEX

Someone ratted us out.

SOAP DISH

Butter Knife.

PEX

Talk about a dead end.

The Mutant Rats slowly stalk towards their prey. From the other end of the corridor, the deadly robot cleaner approaches.

PEX (CONT'D)

Be brave.

SOAP DISH

Kangs *are* brave. Kangs *are* bold. Kangs are-

SILVER

Nothing but trouble.

Pex and Soap Dish look up to see Silver on a catwalk above the park.

SILVER (CONT'D)

So you're the ones who have been sticking their noses into our business.

Pex aims his blaster at Silver.

SILVER (CONT'D)

That would be a very unwise course of

action.

SOAP DISH

My sister is unalive because of you.

SILVER

Now why would I kill my customers?

SOAP DISH

I'm going take you to the cleaners.

Silver laughs.

SILVER

You first.

The robot cleaner advances with deadly intent.

Silver whistles a command and the rats leap forward.

Pex pushes Soap Dish out of the way. The rats scurry to attack again. Pex rolls onto his back and with his blaster fires two shots up into the catwalk.

Silver dives for cover. Pex fires again. The catwalk supports explode and a section of the catwalk falls pinning a rat!

The robot cleaner charges forwards, the spinning blades lunging for Pex and Soap Dish.

SOAP DISH

Move!

They dive in separate directions as the Cleaner moves between them. Soap Dish jumps onto a bench and then FLIPS back onto the Cleaner! She pulls off a panel and starts pulling at the wires within.

Pex keeps firing up onto the catwalk as Silver gets to his feet. Silver whistles again.

The remaining rat, nuzzling its dead mate, turns once again to Pex. It snarls. Yellowing but nevertheless deadly teeth gnash. The creature lunges-

Pex turns and with a single blaster bolt kills the rat stone dead.

SILVER

Damn you both!

Silver taps on his wrist device. A wall section slides away allowing two more cleaners to roll into the square.

Pex turns to shoot - Soap Dish grabs onto his arm. She's stood in the robot cleaners bin, steering it like a chariot.

SOAP DISH

Can't win. Make all speed!

PEX

Okay.

Pex jumps onto the back of the robot cleaner as it speeds forward, the others in hot pursuit.

INT. THE STREETS OF PARADISE TOWERS - DAY

The robot cleaner speeds along the empty corridors.

PEX

Look at this! More of those packages. If we take these to the chief, the game will be over!

...But the other robot cleaners are catching up.

SOAP DISH

Big if!

PEX

Don't worry, I'll handle them.

Pex turns and opens fire. His laser blasts bounce off the robots.

PEX (CONT'D)

Armour plating!

They speed around a corner-

Narrowly missing a pair of Rezzie's who dive into a pile of bin bags for cover.

SOAP DISH

Sorry!

The robot cleaners close in. Their spinning blades cut at the bin.

Pex yanks open another panel on the back of the robot cleaner. Inside the panel are two plastic pipes filled with cleaning liquids... Pex yanks out one of pipes, and soap squirts out of it.

PEX

How's this for a spin cycle!

The pursuing robot cleaners hit the soap and skid... they collide into each other!

BOOM!

PEX (CONT'D)

Looks like you're all washed up!

Pex smiles proudly at Soap Dish but she's in no mood for fun. Soap Dish steers them around another corner-

PEX (CONT'D)

Look out!

- A group of caretakers are marching down the corridor.

Soap Dish panics - spins the wheel! The robot cleaner crashes into the wall - topples - Soap Dish and Pex are thrown clear. They land in another pile of trash bags.

CUT TO BLACK.

INT. CRASH CORRIDOR - MOMENTS LATER

FADE IN: A ringing noise as the caretakers pull Pex and Soap Dish from the rubbish heap. The Chief Caretaker is waiting for them.

FWSH! Caretakers attend to the burning wreckage of the cleaning robot with extinguishers.

CHIEF CARETAKER

I should have known you'd be the cause of this mischief. There are strict punishments for joyriding...

The Chief Caretaker holds up a vial.

CHIEF CARETAKER (CONT'D)

There are even stricter punishments for drug peddlers.

PEX

Chief, you don't understand-

CHIEF CARETAKER

Chief. Caretaker.

SOAP DISH

That's not our fyx. We stole it.

CHIEF CARETAKER

So you're thieves as well?

PEX

No! We had the evidence. You have to believe me. We were bringing it to you!

SOAP DISH

You've got the short end of the stick! We can show you where the fyx comes from. No untruths here!

CHIEF CARETAKER

You Kangs have been nothing but trouble ever since we arrived. No respect. No discipline. There are rules for a reason you know-

Pex notices something in the crowd.

CHIEF CARETAKER (CONT'D)

And now you're bringing drugs to *my* fine streets.

PEX

Not us. Them.

Pex nods. The Chief Caretaker turns...

Silver and Bruckheimer, in their full CARETAKER UNIFORMS, are dealing with the burning cleaner.

PEX (CONT'D)

They're the ones behind this.

CHIEF CARETAKER

My caretakers? Responsible for this mess? Nonsense.

PEX

You have to believe us.

CHIEF CARETAKER

I don't want to hear another word! Take them away!

Pex and Soap Dish argue and plead as they are dragged away by armed Caretakers.

Across the corridor, Silver winks at Bruckheimer. The other man is unconvinced, turning away from his partner in crime to hide his doubt.

CUT TO:

INT. DETENTION CELL - NIGHT

Pex pleads with the DEPUTY CHIEF CARETAKER. There are two more guards in the room.

PEX

You have to listen. The Fyx, the rats, the power drain... it's all linked and I can put an end to it.

DEPUTY CHIEF CARETAKER

Power drain? What power drain?

(beat)

How do you know about the power drain?

PEX

No time to explain. We only time for action.

The deputy Chief Caretaker taps his key card, considering his options. Decision made, he slips the key card into his pocket.

DEPUTY CHIEF CARETAKER

It's against regulation. Maybe if you'd tell me who is behind it all I could do something.

PEX

I... I can't.

DEPUTY CHIEF CARETAKER

And what about you miss?

SOAP DISH

No point. Won't listen.

(to Pex)

This is all your fault.

PEX

My fault?

Soap Dish pushes him.

PEX (CONT'D)

Look, I don't hit girls.

Soap Dish keeps pushing him.

SOAP DISH

Cowardly cutlet! Rubber neck! Scared of Kangs! Scared of Caretakers! No good muscle brain! Kangs are brave! Kangs are bold!

Soap Dish leaps on him! The two other Caretakers pull her back. She wrenches free and falls against the Deputy Chief Caretaker. She looks up at him sadly.

SOAP DISH (CONT'D)
...Kangs need you help.

Gently, the caretaker pushes her away.

DEPUTY CHIEF CARETAKER
I'm sorry miss.

He motions to the other Caretakers. The first opens the cell door as the Deputy Chief Caretaker marches out. The two caretakers follow. The cell door slides shut.

PEX
...I was trying to help you.

SOAP DISH
I know. I spoke untruths. You're not so bad for a muscle-brain.

PEX
Then why did you say all those mean things?

Soap Dish turns, the Deputy Chief Caretaker's key card in her hand. She smiles mischievously.

SOAP DISH
Getting us an outway.

CUT TO:

INT. SECRET DRUG LABORATORY - NIGHT

CRASH! Bruckheimer smashes lab equipment, sweeping vials onto the floor. With a primal roar he picks up a metal pipe, raising it above his head-

Silver grabs the pipe with a firm hand.

SILVER

What do you think you're doing!

BRUCKHEIMER

It's over. Can't you see that? They'll tell the chief caretaker everything.

SILVER

I didn't escape that stupid war to be undone by a lunkheaded idiot and that skagrat brat! Stupid meddling kids!

Silver paces the lab - mental cogs grinding out malicious thoughts.

SILVER (CONT'D)

This can still work. Take everything we have, dump it into the water supply. We'll get them all hooked... then I'll be in control.

BRUCKHEIMER

You?

SILVER

Who else?

Bruckheimer scoffs - a dawning realisation.

BRUCKHEIMER

Of course. This was always the plan. You used me.

Silver looks around.

SILVER

Where are the vats?

BRUCKHEIMER

I already destroyed them.

SILVER

You what?!

BRUCKHEIMER

Incinerated them. I'm not going down for you.

(beat)

And I won't let you hurt my rats any more.

SILVER

Your rats? Ha! You may be their

creator... but you are not their master.

Silver whistles. Two of the mutant rats stalk menacingly into the room.

SILVER (CONT'D)
I could have ruled in Paradise.
(sighs)
Now I'll just have to destroy it instead.

He whistles again and the rats leap forward. Bruckheimer screams!

CUT TO:

INT. POWER PLANT CONTROL ROOM - NIGHT

Pex and Soap Dish race into the power plant, weapons primed.

PEX
You said you followed a caretaker but he disappeared?

SOAP DISH
Thin air!

PEX
Then there must be a secret door.

SOAP DISH
Of course! The Great Architect built lots

of out of sight ways. Kangs use them, mayhaps fixers use them too!

Soap Dish starts tapping on the wall. She finds a hollow point.

SOAP DISH (CONT'D)

Here.

Pex wrenches a metal pipe from the wall and starts to SMASH at the concrete.

INT. SECRET STAIRWAY - NIGHT

Pex and Soap Dish descends a secret staircase.

INT. SECRET DRUG LABORATORY - NIGHT

Pex and Soap Dish rush into the laboratory. Silver is working on a device. He doesn't seem surprised to see them.

SILVER

Of course. I should have known that idiot calling himself 'Chief Caretaker' couldn't keep you locked up. He can barely keep the lights on.

PEX

That's because you've been stealing power. Using it to make your sick creatures.

SILVER

Surprisingly astute of you.

PEX

I'm here to put an end to you villain.

SILVER

Ha! I'm a trained soldier. You're just a boy with a toy and delusions of grandeur.

SOAP DISH

If you're a solider, why didn't you go to war?

SILVER

That was no war. It was suicide and I'm no loser. Not like these crusty old Caretakers. Paradise Towers is falling apart. But I could have been king. One I got you all hooekd on Fyx I would-

SOAP DISH

Yawny.

SILVER

What?

SOAP DISH

Talk too much.

SILVER

You're as impudent as Butter Knife said you were.

BUTTER KNIFE

Deal with her later?

SILVER

Why wait? She's right here.

Butter Knife emerges from the shadows. Her eyes glint like a sharpened blade, ready to strike.

BUTTER KNIFE

If I get all the other Kangs fyxed, Silver will give me all I want. Then I'll be number one, top of the Kangs. I need my hit.

SOAP DISH

I've got a hit right here.

Soap Dish fires at Butter Knife. The other Kang moves with surprising speed.

SILVER

Fyx isn't the only black market drug I brought from the war. This one gives you strength, agility.

Butter Knife grabs Soap Dish by the neck. Close on Butter Knife's eyes - they are bloodshot, flecked with violent hues.

SILVER (CONT'D)
Now if you'll excuse me. I've got something else which is going to blow you away!

Silver picks up the device and runs into the shadows.

Pex points his blaster at Butter Knife but she lifts Soap Dish in front of her, using her as a shield.

SOAP DISH
Stop him! I've got this!

Pex hesitates...

SOAP DISH (CONT'D)
Pex! Go!

Pex chases after Silver.

INT. POWER PLANT - NIGHT

This is the core of the power plant, a large reactor in the centre of Paradise Towers. Energy crackles and pulses. Silver climbs a ladder, the device strapped to his back.

PEX

Stop right there!

Silver looks down to see Pex climbing after him. Silver steps onto a platform and fires two shots at Pex.

SILVER

Damn you!

Pex swings to the other side of the ladder but drops his blaster in the process.

Silver grimaces, then takes the device from his back and attaches it to NUCLEAR POWER CORE. A screen on the device flickers to life. 3 Minutes... and counting!

Silver turns as Pex climbs up onto the platform behind him.

PEX

What are you doing?

SILVER

I'm going to blow this place out of the universe. If I can't have Paradise... Neither can you!

PEX

What, everything's broken and you can't

fyx it?

SILVER

That stupid Kang doesn't realise the drugs are gone. But then again... Butter Knives never were that sharp.

CUT TO:

INT. SECRET DRUG LABORATORY - NIGHT

SMASH! Butter Knife hurls Soap Dish across the laboratory. Soap Dish picks herself up, spitting blood onto the floor.

SOAP DISH

This isn't you. It's the drugs. I don't want to hurt you.

BUTTER KNIFE

You'll take the drugs away. Cold cuts!

Soap Dish tackles Butter Knife but the other Kang picks her up and drops her onto a laboratory table. Soap Dish kicks out and rolls onto the floor.

SOAP DISH

Stop it!

Soap Dish throws a laboratory flask at Butter Knife. Butter Knife's reflexes are super sharp

- she ducks the flask and in one fluid movement pounces at Soap Dish.

Soap Dish barely sidesteps her in time and Butter Knife crashes into a pile of barrels. They clatter to the floor.

Soap Dish slides for her Arrow Gun...

Butter Knife picks herself up and turns as Soap Dish fires two arrows at her. The arrows miss their target but strike the barrels.

Butter Knife smacks the arrow gun from Soap Dish. Soap Dish falls to the floor. She backs away from Butter Knife.

SOAP DISH (CONT'D)

You trust him over a Kang? He's a snake tongue, nothing but untruths!

BUTTER KNIFE

He's going to Fyx me up!

SOAP DISH

(sadly)

No! You're too broken.

INT. POWER PLANT - NIGHT

Silver lunges at Pex. The two men grapple over

the power core. The clock ticks down. 2 minutes 30 seconds and counting.

PEX

Turn it off!

SILVER

You're not afraid to die, are you?

Pex breaks free of Silver's hold. With two clubbed fists he beats down on Silver. Grimacing, Silver kicks out - Pex falls. Silver scrambles to his feet.

SILVER (CONT'D)

Not that you can call Paradise Towers living. You're all just waiting for oblivion. I'm just speeding up the process!

Pex lunges from his crouched position. He tackles Silver - they both go over the edge!

Two minutes and counting.

CUT TO:

INT. SECRET DRUG LABORATORY - NIGHT

Butter Knife falls with her entire weight onto Soap Dish, her hands grabbing Soap Dish's neck. Soap Dish tries to fight free but she can't, the other Kang, pumped full of Silver's poison, is too strong.

Soap Dish reaches out towards the tumbled barrels. One of her arrows is embedded into it...

BUTTER KNIFE

I told him... Butter Knife wouldn't melt. Just give me my Fyx...

Soap Dish's hand grasps the arrow. She pulls!

SOAP DISH

Fix this!

The arrow breaks - Soap Dish digs the arrow into Butter Knife's arm. Yowling in pain the other Kang rolls off her.

Soap Dish runs for the medical cabinet. She opens it. Inside, an injector and vials of DOWNGRADES. She quickly loads the vial into the injector. Her hands fumble...

Butter Knife is back. She wrenches Soap Dish round to face her. The vial flies from Soap Dish's hand... Butter Knife lifts her up by the collar.

BUTTER KNIFE

Going to take you down!

Soap Dish jabs the injector into Butter Knife's neck.

SOAP DISH
You first.

She fires the downgrade into Butter Knife. The effect is instant - the blood rage disappears her eyes, the strenght flees from her eyes. The two Kangs collapse to the floor.

SOAP DISH (CONT'D)
Be alive. Be alive.

Butter knife isn't moving.

SOAP DISH (CONT'D)
Won't lose you. Find a way back.

She clings Butter Knife close to her. Suddenly Butter Knife bursts into life... and tears.

BUTTER KNIFE
Wasn't myself.

SOAP DISH
It's okay. Everything's going to be okay.

CUT TO:

INT. POWER PLANT - NIGHT

One minute and counting.

Pex and Silver hang from electrical cables underneath the platform. Pex struggles to climb back onto the platform.

Silver grabs his boot, yanking hard. Pex almost loses his grip. Silver slowly climbs up Pex's leg.

SILVER

You're stronger than I gave you credit. Could have used you... been my enforcer.

PEX

Not interested.

Forty seconds and counting. Silver grabs at a cable to give himself more leverage. The cable comes loose from it's anchor. Sparks fly as the charged cable dances freely. Pex tries to haul himself up onto the platform.

SILVER

I'd have got you all the drugs and girls you like.

PEX

That's not how I get my kicks... But this is how you get yours!

Pex kicks hard. Silver falls. The cables snag, wrapping around Silver's neck. He struggles desperately as Pex climbs up onto the platform.

Twenty seconds and counting.

Pex crawls towards the device. Three cables run into it. RED, BLUE and YELLOW.

PEX (CONT'D)

Have to turn it off!

Ten seconds and counting.

Pex's hands hover over the device. He makes a choice... He yanks all three cables at once.

One second. The clock stops.

Pex sits heavily on the platform, wiping sweat from his brow. He takes a second to rest then leans over the edge of the platform. Silver has wrestled free and is climbing is way back up the cables.

Pex reaches out a hand.

PEX (CONT'D)

Let me help you!

SILVER

Help me?

PEX

I set the world of Paradise Towers to rights... and this is the right thing to do.

SILVER

You really do believe that nonsense don't you?

Silver slips. Pex strains to reach out further.

PEX

Take my hand.

SILVER

Fine...

Silver reaches out.

SILVER (CONT'D)

On second thoughts, I'll take you with me!

The hidden knife slides out of his sleeve... as the loose electrical cable swings towards him. It hits the knife and the electrical charge sends Silver falling down into the abyss below...

PEX

What a shock!

FADE TO:

INT. FOUNTAINS OF HAPPINESS SQUARE - DAY

Pex and Soap Dish sit on the edge of a fountain. She punches him playfully on the arm.

PEX

Is your friend going to be okay?

SOAP DISH

She's going cold cuts but Blanche is helping her through it.

Pex looks out thoughtfully, as if he is speaking directly to us.

PEX

Drugs aren't the solution. They're the problem! Say no to drugs and yes to life. That's the greatest adventure of them all.

(to Soap Dish)

Hey, mayhaps you could come on another adventure with me? It sure was a wild ride!

SOAP DISH

That Fyx broke a lot of Kangs. They need my help. But you're going to be okay. You're not such a rubber neck after all.

She kisses him on the cheek.

PEX

What was that for?

SOAP DISH

Luck.

She gets to her feet as the Chief Caretaker approaches.

SOAP DISH (CONT'D)

Looks like we're going to need it.

Pex jumps to his feet.

PEX

Chief.

CHIEF CARETAKER

It's Chief Care- oh never mind. I... owe you an apology. And my sincerest gratitude Pex. We all do.

PEX

That's alright Chief. You can always count on me to put the world of Paradise Towers to rights.

CHIEF CARETAKER

And the Caretakers will let you get on with it. So long as you don't break any rules of course. Bide thee well.

The Chief Caretaker salutes and walks away.

SOAP DISH

What a dodge!

PEX

Well I guess this is farewell.

SOAP DISH

It's a shame you won't break the rules anymore. Not even a little bit...

PEX

Why's that?

SOAP DISH

Because I might have time for one more wild ride after all.

He turns towards her, a smile growing on his face.

CUT TO:

INT. CORRIDORS OF PARADISE CITY - DAY

A robot cleaner speeds down the corridor streets of the city, Pex and Soap Dish riding behind it from the bin.

PEX

Woo-hoo!

CUT TO BLACK.

INT. SUB LEVELS - NIGHT [POST-CREDIT STING]

FADE IN. A robot cleaner trundles along the sub levels pulling a wheeled bin behind it. In the bin: SILVER, bloodied and broken.

SILVER

Where... am I?

The robot cleaner comes to a halt before a large metallic door. The door slides open. In the darkness, two large eyes.

MYSTERIOUS VOICE

Hungry...

Silver screams.

CUT TO BLACK.

[NOTE TO PRODUCER: Is it too early to start talking sequel ideas? I've got a great pitch for PEX LIVES!]